IS IT *REALLY* ONLY A MOVIE?

As we rode along, I thought about the dinosaur, and the way he walked, and thoughts spun through my head like pinwheels in a blue norther. The Tyrannosaurus Rex had moved smooth, all right, but slightly mechanical, and had I heard a sort of hum as he crossed the road, like the soft buzz of a battery-powered watch?

Probably not. But I had dreamed off and on that there were these many-tentacled, bladdery, eyes-on-stalks aliens that were doing this to us, making us the stars of low-budget movies they were filming. And if my dreams were, as I suspected, more than dreams, were in fact my tapping into their thought processes, then they could be doing to us again what they had done with us in the drive-in. Didn't low-budget movies nearly always show as part of a double feature?

THE
DRIVE-IN 2
(Not Just One of Them Sequels)

Joe R. Lansdale

BANTAM BOOKS
NEW YORK · TORONTO · LONDON · SYDNEY · AUCKLAND

THE DRIVE-IN 2

A Bantam Spectra Book / July 1989

ISBN 0-553-27905-X

Published simultaneously in the United States and Canada

*Bantam Books are published by Bantam Books, a division of Bantam
Doubleday Dell Publishing Group, Inc. Its trademark, consisting of
the words "Bantam Books" and the portrayal of a rooster, is
Registered in U.S. Patent and Trademark Office and in other
countries. Marca Registrada. Bantam Books, 666 Fifth Avenue, New
York, New York 10103.*

PRINTED IN THE UNITED STATES OF AMERICA

O   0 9 8 7 6 5 4 3 2 1

*This dog-and-pony show is dedicated
with love and respect to that smart writer-gal
from Texarkana, Texas, current of Gulfport, Mississippi,
Mignon Glass.*

Acknowledgments are in order for Jeff Banks, Keith Hamrick, Jerry Heilman, Gary Raisor, David Webb, Ed Gorman, Dean Koontz, Neal Barrett, Lew Shiner, Karen Lansdale, Pat LoBrutto, and "The Hungry Guys" (you know who you are) for their encouragement and/or helpful criticisms. And, of course, a whole lot of credit must be given to me, my own self, because I had to write the sonofabitch.

I'd also like to note, that though part of this novel takes place in my hometown of Nacogdoches, Texas—and I stand by my comments both pro and negative about the place— the scene with the firemen and the burning frat house is purely imaginative. I went for the broad and the comic, and I have nothing but the highest regard and respect for our fire department and its underpaid personnel. I like old houses too. Frats I'll have to think about.

Everything human is pathetic. The secret source of Humor itself is not joy but sorrow. There is no humor in heaven.

MARK TWAIN
Pudd'nhead Wilson

THE
DRIVE-IN 2

Fade-in/Prologue

Pay attention. When I'm through there will be a test.

One day suddenly you're out of high school, happy as a grub in shit, waking up with a hard-on and spending your days sitting around in your pee-stained underwear with your feet propped up next to the air conditioner vent with cool air blowing on your nuts, and the next goddamn thing you know, you're crucified.

And I don't mean symbolically. I'm talking nails in the paws and wood splinters in the ass, sore hands and feet and screams and a wavering attitude about the human race. It's the sort of thing that when it happens to you, you have a hard time believing ol' Jesus could have been all that forgiving about it.

It hurts.

Had I been J.C., I'd have come back from the dead madder than a badger with turpentined balls, and there wouldn't have been any of this peace-and-love shit, and I would have forgotten how to do trivial crap like turn water to wine and multiply bread and fishes. I'd have made myself big as the universe and made me two bricks just the right size, and I'd have gotten the world between the bricks, and *whammo*, shit jelly.

1

It wouldn't do to make me a messiah. I've got a bad attitude.

I do now, anyway.

It isn't that I expected life to be so sweet and fine that I'd grow up sweating pearls and farting peach blossoms, nor was I expecting to live to be three million and have endless fan mail from long-legged, sex-starved Hollywood starlets telling me how they'd like to ravish my body and bronze my pecker. But on the other hand, I was expecting a little better than this.

Me and my friends went to the drive-in to see movies, not to become part of them.

The evening we drove into the Orbit things started going to hell in a fiery hand-basket. We had just gotten settled in, and this big, red comet came hurtling from the sky like a tomato thrown by God, and then the comet split apart and smiled rows of saw-bladed teeth at us.

And when I thought the comet would hit us and splatter us into little sparklers of light, it veered upwards and moved out of sight. What it left in its wake was some bad business.

The drive-in still had light, but the light came from the projectors and the projectors didn't seem to have any source of electricity. We were surrounded by a blackness so complete it was like being in a bag with a handful of penlights. The blackness beyond the drive-in was acidic. I'll never forget what it did to that carload of fat people that drove off into it (or what I assumed it did), or the cowboy who put his arm into it and got his entire self dissolved.

Anyway, we were trapped.

Things got nasty.

There was nothing to eat in the drive-in besides the concession food, which was bad enough, but when that got low, people started eating one another, cooked and un-cooked.

Then two of my friends, whacked out from lack of food, got hit by this strange blue lightning (Randy was riding on Willard's back at the time) and it fused them together and made them uglier than a shopping mall parking lot and gave them strange powers and they became known as the Popcorn King. They weren't friends of mine and Bob's anymore. They weren't anyone's friends. They were now one creature. A bad creature.

Hello, permanent blue Monday.

The Popcorn King used his weird powers and unlimited popcorn to control the hungry crowd, and Bob and I might have joined them if it hadn't been for the jerky stash Bob had in his camper truck. The meat kept us from having to eat the King's popcorn, which had grown kind of funky, and from having to eat other folks, which was a thing the King encouraged.

But me and Bob were realistic enough to figure eating other folks and each other was just on the horizon, so to speak, so we decided, live or die, we were going to destroy the Popcorn King, and we did, with the help of this evangelist named Sam and his wife, Mable, who we thought was dead at the time. But that's another story and I've already told it. Let me just say that Sam and Mable together probably had a lower IQ than the foreskin on my dick.

To shorten this all up, we killed the Popcorn King, smashed him with a bus and blew his ass up, and for our efforts, Samaritan as they were, the King's followers stripped us naked, called us some real bad names, crucified us and started building bonfires at the bottom of our crosses so they could have us for lunch.

Then the comet decided to come back.

The big red bastard couldn't come back before we were crucified. No sir. It had to wait until we were up on those crosses with nails in our hands and feet and our bare asses hanging out before it chose to make an appearance.

But, I suppose I shouldn't complain. The bonfire didn't get built, and consequently, we didn't get eaten.

The comet did what it had done before, only this time when it went away the blackness around the drive-in went with it and folks got in their cars and trucks and drove off.

A fella named Crier, who was kind of a friend of ours, but who was planning on eating us if we got cooked, took us down from the crosses. Mable, who got crucified with us and was really dead this time, wound up burned and buried under some lumber left over from where the concession exploded while we were in the process of killing the Popcorn King. Sam died shortly after all this, about the time he got loaded in the back of the camper, but I didn't know this at the time.

Crier had to help me and Bob to the truck, and Bob got put in the back with Sam, and I rode up front with Crier, who did the driving. My feet weren't in any condition to push pedals. Getting crucified is not like stepping on a sticker or having a splinter in your palm, I'll guarantee you. It takes the rhythm out of your step and saps your will to clap to inner music.

So Crier drove us out of there, and at first things looked fine as the missionary position, but when we saw that the highway was buckling and cracking and grass was growing up between the cracks and on either side of the concrete was thick jungle, none of us had to be a nuclear physicist to know things still hadn't gone back to normal. And while we were contemplating this, letting those old inner wheels turn and squeak, a Tyrannosaurus Rex came goose-stepping out of the jungle on one side of the highway, looked at us with contempt, and disappeared into the foliage on the other side.

It was an exhilarating experience. Scary too.

And that's where this part of my story takes up.

SHOWTIME

FIRST REEL

(A Burial, a Tree House, a Burned
Man,
and Titties Close Up)

1

There was some nice scenery out there. Big trees that climbed to a sky bluer than a Swede's eye, and next to the highway was some grass growing so tall and sharp it looked like green spikes.

After being cooped up in that drive-in for who knows how long with the tar-colored sky overhead and people so close together you couldn't scratch your ass without elbowing your neighbor, I suppose I should have been grateful. No one was trying to crucify and eat me, and that was worth something, but even with everything so pretty, it had a sort of landscaped look about it that I couldn't explain. You know, like a movie set that could afford to use real trees and grass and what looked like a real sky but struck me as a little too blue and perfect. It put me in mind of an old woodcut I saw in an art magazine once. The woodcut was from the sixteenth century, I think, maybe earlier, and there was this monk on his hands and knees and he was poking his head through the fabric of a night sky and looking at all manner of gears and machinery on the other side, stuff that made the world work, that swung the sun and moon across the sky and popped out the stars and turned things light or dark.

As we rode along, I thought about the dinosaur, and the way he walked, and thoughts spun through my head like pinwheels in a blue norther. The Tyrannosaurus Rex had moved smooth, all right, but slightly mechanical, and had I heard a sort of hum as he crossed the road, like the soft buzz of a battery-powered watch?

Probably not. But I had dreamed off and on that there were these many-tentacled, bladdery, eyes-on-stalks aliens that were doing this to us, making us the stars of low-budget movies they were filming. And if my dreams were, as I suspected, more than dreams, were in fact my tapping into their thought processes, then they could be doing to us again what they had done with us in the drive-in. Didn't low-budget movies nearly always show as part of a double feature?

Odder than the dreams was me wanting to see someone. Meaning not someone from the drive-in. They were on my shit list. But I wanted to see someone out there, someone who could make me feel this was more than a movie set. I think I might have felt better if I'd at least seen some beer cans or Frito wrappers lying out beside the road or thrown up in the trees. It would assure me that humanity was out there, ready to start fucking up anything it could get its hands on. There's nothing like pristine wilderness to incite in human beings the need to start chopping down trees, tromping grass, killing animals and throwing down beer cans, so I was pretty certain there wasn't a human being within a hundred miles of us.

Not counting the folks who left the drive-in ahead of us, of course. They hadn't had time to respond to natural tendencies, and after our ordeal, it was doubtful anyone had a beer can or a wrapper to toss. Everything that could be eaten or drunk had been consumed at the drive-in and the containers and wrappers tossed down there.

So the people ahead of us were forced to fight their instincts to litter, though I figured in time the urge would become too strong, and they'd start throwing their clothes out, or pulling over to the side of the road to burn their spare tires and leave the blackened, rubber-dotted rims to mark their passing.

We drove on for quite a time, and when it was getting near dark, Crier said, "Think we ought to find a place to hole up for the night?"

"I doubt we're going to come across many motels," I said.

The sun was going down in what struck me as the north, and I mention this because when we went into the drive-in the highway ran north and south, and when we came out we were heading in what was formerly a northerly direction. But being a creature of habit, and not wishing to give any alien movie-makers the satisfaction of letting on I noticed, I reoriented myself and called the direction in which the sun was falling west.

Besides, you never knew when someone might ask you directions.

Crier found a place off the highway where the jungle cleared out and there was some tall grass that went on for a ways, and he pulled over and parked, came around and helped me out of the truck.

My feet were sore and stiff from the crucifixion and I couldn't walk, but I could lean a little when propped against the camper.

As our duds had been stripped off us by the mad drive-in crowd, Crier had cut holes in blankets for me, Bob and Sam, and slipped them over our heads to serve as clothes, and I took this moment to lift my stylish wardrobe's hem and take a whiz.

Crier went around and opened the back of the camper and helped Bob out, and that's when Crier and I found out about Sam.

"We hadn't no more than gotten started back there," Bob said, "when he snorted once, shit on himself and went on to glory. Or wherever assholes like him go. I won't miss him."

Bob was sentimental like that.

When Crier got Bob propped up next to me, Bob lifted his blanket and took a leak too. If I had waited a minute or two, we could have gone together.

Crier had gone back to the rear of the camper, and Bob called to him, "I know it's a bother, and I hate to ask, you having been so nice to us and all, but—"

"Would I clean Sam's shit out of the back?" Crier said.

"And they say there's no evidence for ESP," Bob said.

Crier took Sam by the heels and dragged him bumpity-bumpity out of the camper and onto the ground. Sam hit hard enough to make me wince. Crier pulled him over to the grass and dropped his hold on the old boy's heels. He peeled Sam's blanket off and went back to the truck and used it to clean the mess up as best he could. It still wasn't going to smell like the perfume counter at J.C.Penney's back there, but it had to beat leaving things the way they were.

Bob began to ease down so he could sit, and I did the same. We managed our legs out in front of us without wincing and moaning too awful much.

Bob looked over at Sam's body in the grass and made a clucking sound with his tongue. "Hell of a thing, ain't it Jack? Life's hard, then you die, then you shit yourself. There's just no dignity in dying, no matter how you look at it."

"Might not be any dignity," I said. "But at least you don't have to get phone calls from aluminum siding salesmen anymore."

"Got news for you," Bob said. "We won't be getting those anyway, and we're alive."

"It's because we don't have a phone," I said. "If we come across a phone, you can bet we'll be hearing from them."

Bob called to Crier. "You're gonna bury the old fart, ain't you?"

Crier came around from the back of the camper. He was a sight. He was scrawny as a month-old corpse, but didn't have as nice a complexion. He still had his clothes and shoes, but they seemed to be held together by little more than body odor and hope. His hair was long and shaggy and thinning. His beard looked like a nest. He had the shit-stained blanket in his hand, and he gracelessly tossed it into the grass, an act that gave me some hope. Humanity was once again on the roll.

"You're kind of pushy, Bob," Crier said.

"I ain't saying you have to bury him—"

"That's big of you."

"—I'm suggesting it. If I had two good hands and two good feet, I might do it."

"Uh-huh."

"Let your conscience be your guide."

Crier said something under his breath, then went to the back of the truck and came out with a tire tool.

"Hey, forget it," Bob said.

Crier used the tool to pop the hubcap off the rear right tire. He took the cap out to the grass and tossed it down next to Sam. He began pulling the grass and cussing while he did it. It was pretty interesting to watch. Once in a while he'd toss a wad of grass, dirty roots still intact, toward Bob, and it would land near his sore feet or slam into the truck beside him. Bob started moving his head like a nervous anaconda.

Actually, I think Crier could have hit him if he'd wanted to. It wasn't that far a shot. Instead, he was trying to make Bob nervous, which I could kind of understand. Bob didn't always bring out the best in a person.

As for me, I tried to sit casual with my punctured biscuit hooks in my lap, looking at the crusty wounds on the backs of my hands where the nails had come out and gone into the wood of my cross.

When Crier had a good patch of grass pulled, he took the hubcap and used it to dig with and his mouth to cuss with. He worked the dirt between his legs like a dog burying a bone.

It was almost solid dark when he finished the grave. It wasn't much, more of a shallow trench, really. The moon came up in the north, right where the sun had gone down, the place I had decided to call west before, and I had a vision of my real or imagined multiple-eyed, many-tentacled, bladder-shaped aliens pulling levers and pushing buttons and causing gears to creak and crank and start the final descent of the sun and the rise of the moon, which spilled its light into Sam's final resting place like thin cream.

Crier hooked his hands under Sam's chin and pulled him over to the trench. Sam's body rustled through the grass like a snake. Crier rolled him into the hole face first. Sam's legs stuck out at one end, and his left arm flopped from the grave and lay in a manner that suggested he was about to push up and get out of that hole as soon as he gathered his strength.

"You're gonna have to dig some more," Bob said.

Crier turned slowly and looked at Bob. The moonlight on his face made him look like the man most likely not to give an ax. I hoped he knew that Bob's sentiments were his own and that I was an independent.

"Maybe not," Bob said. "Hell, just throw some of that grass over the spots that don't fit, and fuck it."

Crier turned back to his work, took hold of Sam's free arm and brutally twisted it behind Sam's back like a kid working his end of a wishbone. When the arm cracked loud enough to run a cold tremor up my spine, Crier pushed it down against Sam's back and put a foot on it and pressed, rocking back and forth on it until it stayed in place. He bent Sam's overlong legs at the knee, folded them to where the soles of his feet touched the back of his naked thighs, sat on them and bounced hard.

Every time Crier got up to examine his handiwork, the legs would creep up slowly. Finally Crier had had enough. He hopped on them one last time, got up and grabbed the hubcap and started scraping the dirt into the trench and topped it off by tossing loose grass on it.

I guess it was an okay grave, in that it beat lying naked in the grass with a blanket full of your shit nearby, but it was disconcerting to see the top of Sam's feet and part of his ankles sticking up in the moonlight. If any of Sam's relatives had been around, I don't think they'd have liked it.

I suppose it got to Crier too, because he took the hubcap and set it on the soles of Sam's feet as a kind of marker. And though it wasn't perfect, it did sort of tidy things up.

Without saying a word, Crier went around on the other side of the truck and got in. I could tell from the way the truck moved he had lain down in the seat.

Bob leaned over to me and said, "Think it would be okay if I asked him to help us into the camper?"

"Maybe not just now," I said.

From inside the cab we heard Crier say something about "goddamn ingrates," and Bob and I went very, very quiet.

2

We crawled under the truck and tried to sleep. The grass made it pretty soft, but there were bugs crawling on me and it began to get cold and I was feeling stiff in the hands and feet. One thing I had gotten used to in the drive-in was the constant moderate temperature, and that made the chill seem even chillier.

I got one of the larger bugs off of me and crushed it with my thumb and forefinger, a movement that made my sore hand throb. The bug's body collapsed like a peanut husk. I tried to look at it closely, but under the truck with only a stray strand of moonlight, there wasn't much to see. It looked like a crushed bug. Maybe I was expecting little silver wires and a battery the size of a pinhead.

I suppose Crier started feeling guilty, because in the middle of the night he came and woke us up and pulled us out from under the truck and helped us into the camper, which he had, in fact, cleaned out quite well, though the odor of Sam's last bad meals clung to the interior like moss.

Still, it wasn't cold in there and the bugs, real or synthetic, weren't crawling or biting.

After we lay down, and Crier was about to shut the back of the camper, Bob said, "No kiss and story?"

Crier held out his hand, palm up, made a fist and let the cobra rise.

Bob looked at Crier's stiff middle finger and said, "That's not nice."

Crier shut the back of the camper and went around to the front seat and lay down.

Bob managed to get up on his knees and thumped his forehead against the glass that connected the camper to the cab.

Crier sat up and turned to look. I've seen more pleasant faces on water moccasins.

"Night-night," Bob said.

Crier did the trick with his finger again, only with less flourish this time, then lay down out of sight.

Bob wiggled onto his sleeping bag, got on his side and looked at me and said, "You know, I like that guy, I really do."

That night the dreams came back, the same sort I'd had in the drive-in. They seemed more like visions than dreams, like I had tapped into some consciousness that controlled things. Bob and Crier didn't have the dreams, so I could only guess that through some quirk of fate, or by alien design, I had been given this gift. Or, I was as crazy as a cat in a dryer.

Hot-wired to aliens or not, the dreams/visions were clear. I could see the aliens in them, their bulbous heads sporting wiggling tendons tipped with eyes, tentacles flashing about, touching gears and punching buttons. Lights and buzzers and beepers going off and on around them. And them leaning forward, conversing with one another in a language that sounded like grunts, squeaks, burps and whines, and yet, a language I could somehow understand.

And some of the things they were saying went like this:

"Slow, uh-huh, uh-huh . . . that's it."

"Nice, nice . . ."

"Very pretty, oh yes, very pretty . . . tight and easy now . . ."

"All right, that's it. CUT!"

Then the connection was cut as well, and the dream, or whatever it was, ended. The next thing I knew it was morning and Crier had joined us for breakfast, such as it was: a can of sardines that we had taken from Sam's bus before we blew it up.

Afterwards, Crier got us out of the back of the camper and made us take turns walking, him supporting us, so that we could exercise our sore feet. Mine had started to curl like burned tortillas, and Crier said if I didn't make them work, they'd quit on me, and that at best, I'd end up having a couple of lumps that had all the mobility of potted plants.

I believed him. I exercised. So did Bob, though he grumbled about it.

Worst part about the exercise, worse even than the pain, was the thirst. It had been a long time since I had had a drink of water, and of course, this was true of Bob and Crier too. In the drive-in, for a time, we existed on soft drinks, and later on, Bob and I had nothing but the juice from jerky, and now the liquid from sardines.

If that doesn't sound so bad, go out some summer evening and do some kind of hard work, like say hauling hay, then try quenching your thirst with a big glass of soy oil or meat broth.

The bottom line was we were dehydrating, starting to look like flesh-colored plastic stretched over a frame of coat hangers.

"I figure," Crier said, after we got through exercising and were sitting with our backs against the truck, "any place as full of trees and grass and critters as this, ought to have water."

I wasn't so sure. I wouldn't have been surprised to come to what looked like a stream only to discover it was colored glass or rippling cellophane.

We were looking at Sam's grave while we talked, examining his ankles sticking up, his feet wearing the hubcap, and all of a sudden, we grew silent, as if possessed of a hive mind.

"I could have at least spoken some words over him," Crier said.

"And who the hell would you have been talking to?" Bob said. "Sam? He don't give a damn about nothing no more. God? Personally, I'm not real fond of the sonofabitch. Or wouldn't be, if I thought he, she, or it, existed."

I didn't say so, but I was in Bob's camp. Like the drive-in patrons, God was on my shit list. I had tried religion during our stay in the drive-in, and it hadn't exactly been a rewarding experience.

I had decided that if there was a God, he was a cruel sonofabitch to allow the things he allowed. Especially since he claimed his name was synonymous with love. It seemed to me that he was little more than a celestial Jack the Ripper, offering us, his whores, rewards with one hand, smiling and telling us he loved us, while with the other hand he held a shiny, sharp knife, the better with which to disembowel us.

"I don't know what I believe anymore," Crier said, "but I feel I owe the ol' boy some words because he's a human being. It doesn't matter if I'm talking to the wind, or just myself. I didn't give him the best kind of burial, so it's the least I can do. And who knows, if there is some God out there, maybe he'll be listening."

Crier said this soft and solemnlike, and you could

almost hear the organ music in the background. I think Bob
was as affected as I was by Crier's remarks, because he
didn't say anything rude, and something of that sort was
always on the tip of his tongue. A lump, like a crippled frog
trying to make it downhill, moved in my throat.

Crier went over to the grave and looked at the hubcap,
picked it up and looked at the soles of Sam's feet, put the
hubcap back, sighed, looked at the jungle.

"I'm here to say some words about this man, but
nothing much comes to me. I didn't really know the poor
bastard, but from what I could tell, he was about the
dumbest sonofabitch that ever shit over a pair of shoes.

"Still, he was a man, and he deserved better than this.
I'm sorry I couldn't get him buried proper, couldn't get his
feet to stay down, but I did get his arm in the grave, and
that was a job. I hope he rests in peace.

"I'm sorry about his wife, Mable. She wasn't any better
or smarter than he was, from what I could tell, maybe a
damn sight dumber. But I guess she did the best she could,
like all of us. She's back at the drive-in, burned up under
some lumber pieces, just in case you care.

"And listen, God, if you're out there, how about some
relief around here? Lighten up. Things are multiple-
fucked-up, and if anyone can put things straight, it ought to
be you. Right? I mean, you hear what I'm saying? Give us
some sign of good things to come. It would be appreciated.
Okay, that's it. Amen."

Crier walked back to the truck, and about the time he
reached it, the jungle parted and out stepped a nasty
red-and-blue dinosaur that was probably a baby Tyrannosaurus Rex, or something close enough to be a double
cousin to one.

Whatever it was, it stood on big hind legs and held two

puny forelegs in front of itself as if pleading. Its face was mostly teeth.

Toothy sniffed the air delicately, scampered over to the grave, snapped at the hubcap with its mouthful of big, sharp teeth, and managed to gulp it and Sam's feet down with very little chewing.

After a moment, Toothy coughed and spat out the hubcap, which now resembled a wad of aluminum foil. He used one clawed foot to scratch Sam out of the grave the way a chicken might scratch a worm from the dirt, bent and bit into Sam's corpse. With a series of rapid head-flipping motions, he proceeded to gobble the old boy so viciously that pieces of Sam flew out of Toothy's mouth and sprinkled the grass.

Finished with his repast, Toothy eyed us, as if giving the dessert counter a once-over.

We stayed very still. Rocks couldn't have been that still.

He let out a little honk that shook the truck, then started to turn toward the jungle.

A weight watcher, to our relief.

But before he could make a complete turn, he froze, turned his head slightly to the side and acquired a look akin to that of a patient who has just experienced the greased finger of the doctor up his ass. Then with a grunt, Toothy leaned slightly forward and cut a monster fart that was reminiscent of an air horn, but with more tonality.

When the fart was finished and Toothy had adopted a more satisfied and comfortable look, he moved into the jungle and out of sight.

After a moment of silence, Bob said, "Well, Crier, hope that wasn't the sign from God you were waiting for."

3

We drove along for a while, and finally Crier, who had been looking pretty distressed for a time, pulled over and killed the motor.

"What's up?"

"Sam," he said. "I can't get him out of my mind."

"Hell, you buried him, didn't you? Wasn't your fault all you had was a hubcap. And that dinosaur even gave him a musical salute after he ate him. Tomorrow sometime, Sam will be fertilizing a patch of ground. What more could you ask for?"

"Fuck Sam. It's me I'm talking about. I don't want to end up buried alongside the road like that."

"You aren't dead, Crier."

"But I might get that way, and I don't want to end up in some trench next to the highway where something can dig me up and eat me."

"Something doesn't dig you up, the worms are going to take care of you, so what's the difference? Maybe we could just leave you where you lie and save the dinosaurs some digging."

"That's nice. I'm pouring out my heart here and you're making fun. I don't want to be left beside the road and I don't want to be buried beside it neither."

"Perhaps we could arrange for you to be whisked away to heaven."

"I want to be carried to the end of the highway."

"Keep driving, and if we don't run out of gas, that's a wish you'll get. You don't even have to be dead. Have you noticed the gas mileage we're getting? It's got to be super or the gas gauge is fucked."

"Forget the goddamn gas gauge and the mileage, I'm serious here. I get croaked, you guys make sure I get to the end of the highway. Something about that appeals to me. I like the idea of finishing things. Dinosaur eats me there, so be it."

"Crier, if you're dead, it doesn't matter if fifty naked girls with tits like zeppelins are at the end of the highway ready to suck your dick until your balls cave in. You'll still be dead."

"Promise me that should something happen to me you'll make sure I get to the end of the highway to be buried."

"Okay."

"Okay what?"

"If you get killed, I'll see you get to the end of the highway and get buried or cremated or something."

"Not cremated. I don't like that."

"Tried it?"

"Just bury me. I'll make you the same promise if you like."

"Something happens to me, leave me in the bushes. I'll be past caring."

Bob rose up in back and tapped on the glass with an elbow, held out his hands to question why we had stopped.

Crier waved him down, started up the engine and pulled back onto the highway.

"I'm going to talk to Bob about it too," Crier said. "Think he'll do it?"

"Who knows about Bob?" I said.

We finally came to a clearing on the right-hand side of the highway. There was grass, but it wasn't high, and I figured a lot of critters had been grazing on it. In the distance I could see the blue of a great lake. Or what looked like a lake. I still felt as if I were on a movie set. Reality was not to be trusted.

Crier turned off the highway and drove over the grass, and it seemed like it took forever to reach the lake. He parked about six feet from it, jumped out and went belly down on the bank and stuck his face into the water and began to drink.

It was real water.

I opened my door and tried to get out, but it was too far a step and too much pressure on my feet to manage it.

I sat and waited for Crier to finish drinking. If there had been any moisture in my mouth I would have salivated.

When Crier was done he came over and got me out of the truck. The grass was soft and I found I could hobble across it without too much support from Crier.

"I couldn't wait," Crier said. "Sorry."

"I'd have done the same," I said.

The water was cool and sweet, and pretty soon Crier had Bob beside me, then all three of us were lying there on our bellies drinking. I was the first to overdo it. I puked up the water and the sardines on the bank, and Bob and Crier followed shortly thereafter.

We finished puking and went to drinking again, slower this time, and when we were finished, we pulled off what we were wearing and went into the water, Bob and I entering it on elbows and knees, looking like pale alligators.

Waterlogged, we climbed on the bank and lay on our backs and looked at the sky. The sun went down—in the south, go figure—and the lake went dark and the moon rose up—in the south, go figure again—and the water turned the color of molten silver.

After we had talked a while about this and that, Crier said, "I'm one tired sonofabitch, boys. Let's call it a night."

Crier got us in the camper and stood at the tailgate. He said, "I'm in no hurry to leave. I like that water. What say we stick around a while? The highway's out there when we decide to try it again."

Sounded good to me, and I said so.

"Yeah," Bob said. "The idea of going off and leaving all that water doesn't excite me right now. Maybe just because I been thirsty for so long. But yeah, let's wait a while."

Crier nodded and went around to the cab to sleep. I lay down on my bedroll, and for the first time since before the big red comet, I felt a stirring of hope. Or maybe I had drunk too much water.

Whatever, it wasn't so exciting it kept me awake.

4

Next day Crier drove the truck to the other side of the lake, near the jungle, and that became our home. In spite of the water, we hadn't planned to stay as long as we did, but one day rolled into the next.

The jungle provided all kinds of fruit, and in defiance of the age of dinosaurs, all manner of recognizable animals from rabbits to squirrels to monkeys to snakes. All of these were good to eat, but in the beginning we left them alone. Not out of any respect for the lesser species, but simply because we couldn't catch the little bastards and had nothing suitable to kill or trap them with. Also, Bob and I were still crips, and you've got to have legs to run critters down.

Crier made a spear by breaking off a long, thin limb in such a way that it left a point. He put fruit rinds in the lake and stood in the water with them floating around him. He waited for fish to come and nibble at the rinds, then he tried to spear them.

Sometimes it took all day for him to get one, but he stayed with it. He was so determined that sometimes dinosaurs would come and stand off in the distance and watch. I think they were amused.

29

As time went by Crier got better, and later he changed to a more successful method. He got some strong vine and whittled a hook out of wood with a beer can opener he flattened and sharpened with a file from Bob's tool box. He used bugs and worms for bait. By the end of the day, he'd have a pretty nice mess of fish.

I was the fire builder. I'd pull grass and let it dry for a day or two, always keeping the supply ahead of the demand. When the grass looked brittle, I'd take two files from the tool box and knock them together until they made a spark, which I directed into the grass. By blowing on the spark, I could get a blaze going, and then I would feed it twigs, then larger kindling, and finally big hunks of wood. Before long, I'd have a good fire going.

Bob cleaned the fish and cooked them by spitting them on a green limb and hanging the limb between two upright forked sticks. The fish tasted pretty good. Every night, before bed, we ended up with a pile of fish bones and fruit rinds around us.

In time, Bob and I healed, and once we could get around, we turned industrious.

With what we had in the tool box, we managed to make some simple tools for cutting and splitting wood. And damn if we weren't making crude lumber, notching it and pegging it and building a two-story house at the edge of the jungle. It wasn't anything to impress *Better Homes and Gardens*, but it was all right. We managed to use the limbs of this big tree as part of it, and the tree's foliage was so thick the house blended into it. We christened the place Jungle Home. It made me feel like I was a relative of the Swiss Family Robinson. A poor relation, to be sure, but a relation.

The upper floor was the sleeping nest, and by stuffing it with leaves and dried grass and putting the sleeping bags and blankets on top of that, we had a pretty comfortable place.

We also built a deck of split wood and bamboo on either side of the top floor, and it gave us a place to sit and feel the wind.

It wasn't paradise, but it beat being jabbed in the eye with a number two pencil.

But, as a great philosopher once wrote over the urinal in Buddy's Fill-up, "Things will go and change on you."

Crier and Bob had gone off hunting, since Crier had finally made a bow and a few arrows, and from here on out the animal populace was no longer safe. It was going to be roast rabbit and roast squirrel to go with the fish from now on.

Or so said Crier.

I had my doubts, since I had seen Crier practicing with that thing. It didn't look to me that he could have hit the side of a barn with a cannon, let alone a squirrel with a dull arrow. Still, I was hoping for him. I was beginning to tire of fish and fruit, fine as it had once seemed.

Isn't that the way of humans? They're never happy. One day I'm living off sardines and jerky with no water, and the next thing you know, I'm complaining about having fresh water, fish and fruit. Before long, I'd probably want a sauna in Jungle Home and someone to cater my meals.

Anyway, Crier and Bob went off on safari, and I was home filling some water containers we had made out of thick cylinders of hollowed-out bamboo.

I finished the job, stripped off my blanket, and went out and sat on the deck and dangled my feet over the edge.

I had no more than gotten comfortable, when I heard a car out on the highway, the engine straining and knocking as if it were about to explode.

I found me a good spot between the limbs and leaves, zeroed in on the highway, and saw a battered green Galaxy. It was coughing gouts of black smoke from under its hood and pooting a matching concoction from its tailpipe.

The driver hit down on the horn for some reason, and the horn hung.

This wasn't the Galaxy's day.

It slowed, turned off the highway onto the grassland, started weaving and picking up speed again.

I could see a figure in the front seat, fighting the wheel as if it were some rare breed of poisonous hoop snake. Then the driver lost it or quit, because the Galaxy veered to the left toward the lake.

The closer it got to the lake, the more speed it lost. It got down to a crawl. But it still made the water and dipped its nose in. Hot black smoke hissed up in a cloud, and the Galaxy began to slide languidly into the water.

And I was moving.

I had minded my own business so long, I was somewhat surprised when my Good Samaritan urges came back to me like a return bout of malaria fever. I went down the ladder two steps at a time and started running across the grassland toward the lake.

Owing to the gradual slope of the shore, the Galaxy had still not eased all the way in. The back right window was open, and I climbed through that.

The backseat was little more than springs and foam rubber. On the floorboard was something that looked like burnt sticks and brush. Another look and I knew it was human. Its skin was burned the color of neglected bacon. There was no hair, features or genitals. One of its arms was lifted, fingers extended and frozen in a pose that made the hand look like a miniature weed rake.

Water began to trickle in the back window. Already the

front seat was filled. The thing on the floor didn't look alive, so I was about to go over the seat for the driver when the garden rake took hold of my ankle.

I jerked and flesh came off of the ruined hand and ran down my ankle like dirty Jell-O. I looked at the thing and it opened its mouth, made a croaking noise that sounded like "Kill me."

The water would take care of that. I couldn't. I went over the seat and into the water and found the driver, fearing he or she would be like the burned creature on the floorboard.

I got the driver's head out of the water, saw it was a woman. I started pulling her into the backseat by the chin. The rising water helped me.

The car was going under now, and I had time to get one deep breath before the whole kit and caboodle sank to the bottom of the lake.

The mud was stirred up down there and it was like being in creamed coffee. Somehow I got out the open window and tugged the woman after me, tried to kick to the surface.

The woman was deadweight and I couldn't get us up. We sank to the bottom. Since we were near the edge of the lake, it wasn't too deep, so I buried my toes in the sand and flexed my knees and shot us to the surface.

I managed her on shore, rolled her on her stomach, got hold of her arms and worked them some, pausing to push in the middle of her back. She puked.

I turned her over, cleared her mouth with my fingers and started mouth-to-mouth. It was a stinky job and tasted of vomit, but after a short time she coughed hard once and started breathing regularly.

She blinked at me. "Timothy?"

"He the burned guy?"

She nodded.

"He's still down there."

"Best," she said, and tried to get up on her elbows. She looked at that part of my body I least wanted her to look at.

"Small," she said.

"It's cold, for Christsakes."

But she wasn't listening. She had fallen back and was out of it.

5

Considering the way she had insulted my anatomy, I wasn't in any rush to pick her up and carry her to Jungle Home, but I finally gave it a try. She was a pretty hefty gal.

I put her down, went back to Jungle Home, found the keys to the camper and drove over there and got her, loaded her into the back, letting her head bump the tailgate only a couple of times.

When I got her stretched out, I moved her hair out of her face and took my first good look at her. She wasn't bad-looking. Somewhere between eighteen and twenty-one. Guessing ages is not one of my better attributes.

Under the wet clothes her breasts looked nice and so did the width of her hips and the shape of her thighs. I thought about getting her wet clothes off to make her more comfortable, but I feared an ulterior motive.

I left her there in a puddle and went back to Jungle Home, stopping on the way to look at myself in the truck's wing mirror. My hair was wet and twisted and my scraggly little beard looked like a smear of grease. If I was going to have whiskers, why couldn't I have a full set like Bob and Crier.

I did the best I could combing my hair with my fingers,

then went on up to Jungle Home and put on my blanket and tied it around my waist with a belt I had made of vines. Then I lay down on my sleeping bag and found that all that exertion had worn me out. I went right to sleep.

Next thing I knew, Bob and Crier were back. They had a vine basket of fruit, but no game.

"The great hunters return," I said.

"He saw a bunny," Bob said, "and couldn't shoot it. He got all dewy-eyed."

"It had a little pink nose," Crier said. "After all that's happened, I just couldn't kill something."

"Think those fish you catch live happily ever after in our bowel movements?"

"They aren't cute like bunnies," Crier said.

"Boys," I said, "there's a girl down in the camper."

"Don't joke me," Bob said. "I see a fork in a tree and I get hard."

"I'm not joking," I said, and told them the story.

We brought the basket of fruit with us, and when we got around to the back of the camper and looked inside, it was empty. There was a pool of water where she had been and her clothes and tennis shoes were laid out on the tailgate.

"Melted, I figure," Bob said.

"I'm right here."

We turned. She was about ten feet away, wearing only faded blue bikini panties. Her blond hair was dry now and somehow she had combed it out. It fell to her wide shoulders and tumbled over them and, much to our happiness, stopped just before covering her breasts, which were firm and full with areolae the size of half-dollars and the color of warm beef gravy. The nipples were thick and firm, like the tips of pointing fingers. She had a narrow waist and her ribs showed from having lost too much weight. There were faint, pink bands here and there on her body, as if she had been lashed with something. She had her hands on her hips and was looking right at us. If she was embarrassed, I couldn't tell it.

"Christ," she said. "Haven't you boys seen titties before?"

"There's titties," Bob said, "then there's titties."

"This is my first time, ma'am," Crier said. "I've heard of them, of course."

"Fuck with me, any kind of way," she said, "and I'll break your legs off and shove them up your assholes."

"Me first," Crier said.

But the way she looked at us then made us step aside. She came over and got her clothes and started putting them on.

"You boys enjoying the show?"

"Very much, yes," Bob said.

She finished dressing, sat on the tailgate, and looked at us. I guarantee we weren't as pleasant to look at as she was.

She said, "Had a cousin told me about a boyfriend she'd had. Said he was so horny he'd go to the ocean and fuck the water in case there might be a shark out there that had swallowed a girl. Know what she meant now. You could at least close your mouths."

"We're not so bad," Crier said. "We brought you some fruit."

She eyed the fruit we had left on the tailgate and said, "It isn't full of dick holes, is it?"

"Oh, come on," I said, "we're not that bad. All things considered, we're doing okay. We're not trying to rape you, are we? Look here. I'm Jack, this is Bob, and this is Crier."

Her face changed a little then, and there was something behind that pretty skin and those green-gray eyes that wasn't so pretty. But whatever it was went away as quickly as it had arrived.

She took a plumlike fruit from the basket and bit out of it. The juice leaped from it in gold beads and flecked her lips and cheeks and she began to chew. After a moment, she spat out the seed, and went deeper into the fruit like a lion biting the innards out of an antelope's belly. When she finished that one, she ate another.

Somehow, watching her eat was as good as a peep-show. None of us said a word.

When she was finished, she said, "Now you've had a look at my tits and watched me eat. I hope you're happy. Had you showed five minutes earlier, you could have gone off in the bushes with me and watched me pee."

"You could have called us," Bob said.

"Nice dresses," she said, nodding at Bob and me.

"Let's not talk fashion," I said. "Tell us about yourself. Before the drive-in and up to now."

"Why would you want to know?"

"Entertainment," I said. "It's not like we have a pressing social calendar. We know more than we want to know about each other. Give us something new to think about."

"All right," she said. "Sit down and get comfy, because this is going to take a while."

SECOND REEL

(Grace Talks About Frat House Fires,
Raw Liver,
and a Nine Iron to the Noggin)

1

My name is Grace, and I come from a little burg called
Nacogdoches. It's supposed to be the oldest town in Texas.
We got a sign that says so, but it doesn't look that old—the
town, I mean, not the sign.

The place is still kind of neat, but it's going to hell fast,
and when I look at photographs Mom and Dad have of it
twenty-five years ago, it really chaps my highly attractive
ass.

It's one of those towns where the fine old houses and
the massive trees have been torn or cut down so progress
can slither in. You know progress. Burger King, McDonald's, and all manner of plastic eateries where the wrappers
for the burgers and the lettuce inside them taste pretty
much alike, and it's my opinion the wrappers have a more
natural tint than the lettuce and are probably more nutri-
tious.

These days the old houses are gone and you can stand
in the parking lot of McDonald's on North Street and toss
a dried Big Mac underhanded and bounce it off the front
glass of Wendy's on the other side of the street. Or you can
go over to University Drive and toss a pepperoni pizza, no
anchovies, out of the driveway of Mazzio's Pizza and wing
an innocent bystander on the table-laden deck of Arby's.

I went to high school and college in good ol' Nac. The college is called Stephen F. Austin University, and it's named after one of the guys that helped con Texas from Mexico.

I was majoring in anthropology/archaeology, but what I really wanted to be was a karate instructor, since my dad, who was a black belt in kenpo, had been teaching me ever since I was five. If it matters, I'm first degree brown belt now.

But like Dad, I couldn't see any real future in martial arts. Or to be more precise, I think I let Mom convince me there wasn't any future in it. She talked Dad into being a manager of an optical store and she wanted something like that for me, or as she always put it, "Kicking people is all right, but you can't make a decent living at it. You got to have something to fall back on."

Well, I had been hearing this speech since I was old enough to know which was the business end of a tampon, so when I saw this *National Geographic* special on archaeology on television, I thought it might be just what I was looking for.

There were these folks with tans about the color of fresh walnut stains applied to burnt mahogany, wearing khaki shorts and pith helmets, and they were swarming all over these ruins. Fire ants couldn't have been any busier.

They were doing a lot of pointing and writing in notebooks and looking intelligent. There were close-ups of pottery shards from pots that had been made before Jesus was old enough to suck Mary's tit, and there were skull fragments and pieces of bones from the guys and gals that had made the pots.

The show ended with a close-up of this woman with sweat running from under her pith helmet and onto her face and mixing with the sand there, and she was looking

out over these little fragments of walls, looking soulful as a
Baptist preacher, contemplating the past and all the great
civilizations that had arisen there and folded back in on
themselves like a card table.

It was inspiring.

Thinking back on it now, she may have been looking
out over that sand waiting for somebody to pick her up in an
air-conditioned truck and drive her over to a Mideast
Hilton.

But the desire to dig holes in the ground and hold the
bony remains of ancient pottery makers in my hands had
come over me like the Holy Ghost. I couldn't think of
anything else. I checked out archaeology books and read
them cover to cover and started envisioning ancient civilizations marching ghostlike through Nacogdoches, throwing
down pots and bowls and breaking them so I could find
them a zillion years later.

What I didn't get from those books, or refused to get,
was how goddamn hard archaeology is. And it's dirty work.
Those people on *National Geographic* weren't just deeply
tanned, they were downright filthy.

At the end of a day, having sifted through enough sand
to fill Galveston Beach, the sun burning through my clothes
like an X ray, it was hard for me to take a whole lot of pride
in a few broken pieces of pottery that some prehistoric dude
had marked on with a pine needle.

Looking back on it, it was pretty wonderful stuff, I
guess, but I don't like working in the heat and getting so
dirty you have to use a putty knife to get it off your elbows.
And I didn't even have a pith helmet. Just a cap that said
Nacogdoches Dragons on it, and they weren't winning
many ball games.

If someone from *National Geographic* had showed up
right then, I'd have stuffed a year's run of magazines down

their throat and kicked them until they shit a single bound volume.

It's not that I'm a weak sister. I'm not. Karate gave me patience as well as determination. But it's mostly clean work. A little sweat and dirty feet is all. And I did my workouts in our air-conditioned garage or the college gym. If you have to use martial arts on the street, it doesn't take but a few moments to open up a can of whup ass, then you can find some air-conditioned building to cool off in when it's over.

Even indoor archaeology is hard.

On one dig I found some pottery pieces, and I was assigned to try and reconstruct them. That's like giving a blind, crippled monkey a hammer, a bag of nails, and a pile of lumber and telling him to build an A-frame. I'm the gal who still has an unfinished fifty-piece puzzle of a white cat in my closet at home, and I got that puzzle for my tenth birthday.

I'd go to the lab every night and try to do that pottery, and I'll tell you, after fifteen minutes of that I was dangerous. I wanted to kill something and drink a couple of bottles of Nervine.

Bottom line is, I quit. And that was the turning point. Had I stayed in archaeology, I'd probably have been home studying, or up at the lab, destroying my nerves with that pottery instead of meeting up with Timothy and Sue Ellen and tooling on over to the Orbit Drive-in that weird Friday night.

2

So, on the night after I'd given up archaeology and my chance to have something to fall back on, I was out riding around in my old Chevy Nova trying to figure out what I was going to do with the rest of my life, and I'll tell you, what I was coming up with was not pretty.

I thought about all those stories I'd heard about college dropouts and how they spent their lives working behind the counter at K mart or pulling the train for the football team during off season. I could envision myself standing on the corner of North and Main with a cigarette jutting out of my mouth, one side of my lip pulled up in a permanent snarl, and me thinking how I can get a few dollars so I can go over to the 7 Eleven and buy me a bottle of Thunderbird wine. Nothing would be too low for me to do: prostitution, theft, drug-running, murder, working as a used-car salesman. In time I would be shunned by winos and Baptists alike.

On the other hand, I was also thinking about whoever had inherited my prehistoric pottery shards, and I felt a wicked elation that while I was out tooling around, someone was hunched over those shards with their eyes twitching, their hands shaking, wishing I had quietly pushed those fragments down a gopher hole.

45

Anyway, I was riding around, taking back streets mostly, thinking, and I came up on this fire.

There were cars pulled over to the curb and people were standing on the sidewalk and out front of their houses, watching a frat house burn down.

I pulled across from the house, behind the string of parked cars, got out and leaned on the Nova and watched.

The fire department was there and the firemen were jerking hoses, yelling and hopping on the lawn like grass-hoppers. Every now and then one of them would erupt from the doorway of the burning structure like the end result of the Heimlich maneuver, land in the yard on his hands and knees, and crawl about feebly, coughing smoke like a little dragon.

I had never seen a fire like that before, and it didn't take Smokey the Bear to tell me it was some kind of serious. A blazing paper hat would have been easier to save.

While I was watching the frat joint burn up—hating that it was an old house of the sort the city council loved to see go so an aluminum building the shape of a box could take its place, or some concrete could be laid down for a car lot—a tan van came down the street and stopped at the curb and three guys fell out of it yelling. Frats, I figured. Most likely they had gone for a six-pack, or to work their version of heavy machinery, a Trojan dispenser, and had come back to find they had forgot to turn the fire off from under the chili, and now their pad was on its way to becoming air pollution.

Two of them sat on the curb and started crying and the other one rolled around on the lawn and whimpered like a dog with glass in his belly. A fireman came over and yelled at him and kicked him in the butt. The guy crawled off and joined his comrades at the curb and they cried in trio.

I hoped like hell there wasn't anyone inside that house. If so, they wouldn't be graduating.

I was about to leave when I was touched lightly on the elbow and a voice said, "You start this one, baby?"

"Nope. I'm all out of matches."

"Then you got nothing to worry about."

I turned and looked at Timothy. I had known him all my life, had been over to his house to play when we were kids, and he had been over to mine. There had never been anything romantic between us, though when I was twelve I talked him into playing doctor and discovered what I'd heard about boys was true: They were fixed up different from girls.

"Good to see you," I said. "It's been a while."

One of the firemen came coughing out to the curb across from us and sat down next to one of the frat boys. The one who had been rolling on the ground sobbed and said, "They gonna save it?"

The fireman took off his smoke-stained hat, coughed, and looked at the frat the way some people look at retarded children. "Son, we'll be lucky if we save the mineral rights on that sonofabitch."

The three frats really started to cry.

The roof collapsed then and the sparks from it rose up to heaven and turned clear like the souls of fireflies gone off to meet their just rewards.

"Last time I heard," Timothy said, "you were digging holes in the ground or something. Had some night classes too."

"A lab," I said. "Archaeology in the daytime, labs at night. I had to let it go."

Then I told him the whole story.

"I quit too," he said.

"I never knew you started."

"It was the math fixed me. Never could understand how X could be some other number. It always looked like X to me. I couldn't make sense of it. If X was ten one time, how could it be fifteen the next? Who the hell could keep up with what X was if it could be anything?

"What I should have taken was all P.E. courses and majored in golf. I can't make X and Y add up, but by God, I can knock those little white balls to Dallas."

And he could. I had played golf with him before. My golfing style was akin to a frightened matron trying to beat a rat to death with a curtain rod, but I had played enough to know the good stuff when I saw it, and Timothy had the good stuff. A number of pro golfers had made the same observation, and Timothy had mentioned more than once that he was thinking about taking his clubs on the road and seeing what he could do.

"We're on our way to the Orbit," Timothy said. "Want to go?"

"We?"

"Sue Ellen. She loves that horror stuff."

Sue Ellen was Timothy's little sister. She was twelve. Last time I'd seen her was two years back, and she wanted me to explain why Barbie and Ken were smooth all over. I didn't remember having any answers.

"I doubt she even remembers me," I said. "She might feel uncomfortable."

"She remembers you quite well."

"She's sort of young for blood and guts, isn't she?"

"Tell me about it. Mom and Dad think I'm taking her over to see *Bambi*, *Cinderella*, *The Fox and the Hound* and assorted cartoons in a Disney dusk-to-dawn extravaganza."

"Wonder how they got that idea," I said.

I took my car home, told my parents where I was going, not mentioning that Sue Ellen was waiting in the car with Timothy, and we went over there in the Galaxy.

When we got there, the line was as long as the Macy's Thanksgiving parade, and, of course, we got a place near the end of it. The flashing blue-and-white Saturn symbol of the Orbit was far enough away to look like a Ping-Pong ball with an oversized washer around it.

It was warm and the air was full of mosquitoes. Rolling up the windows made you hotter, and rolling them down fed you to the mosquitoes. Timothy talked about giving it up and going home, and I was for it. But not Sue Ellen.

"You promised me, Timmy. You said you'd take me. You know I want to see *The Toolbox Murders*."

I turned and looked at Sue Ellen perched in the middle of the backseat. She was blond and fair and had moist blue eyes and a freckled pug nose and a red bow mouth. Course, it was dark enough you couldn't see all this, but you knew it was there, and telling her no was a lot like kicking a puppy for licking your hand.

"We'll be miserable," Timothy said. "Besides, *The Toolbox Murders*? How'd I let you talk me into that?"

"You promised, Bubba. And if any of it bothers me, you can explain it to me."

"That's choice. I might need you to explain it to me."

"See, I'm old enough."

"One word about mosquitoes, one complaint, and we're out of here."

"Deal."

Had the weather been hotter, the mosquitoes thicker, or if Sue Ellen had had all the charm of Dr. Frankenstein's hunchback assistant, we might have cut for home right then. Sue Ellen would have grown up to break hearts,

Timothy would have gone on to hit little white balls across great expanses of greenery for unreasonable amounts of money, and I might have ended up with my own karate studio.

3

All right, I'm going to stop with Grace's story now. For all you dipshits in the back row who haven't been listening—Leroy, quit playing in that pile of shit. Put that stick down. Yeah, well, screw you too, little buddy. I hope your balls get covered in ants.

Now, all you bozos keep interrupting my reading here and I'm tired of it. You keep saying, "What about the comet? What about the comet?" Well, I've got no new news on the comet, okay? You've heard it all before. I've told you that story half a dozen times. I started this story with the comet. Remember?

No, I don't change it as I go along, Leroy. Look, I don't make you come and listen, do I, huh?

Why did all this happen?

We've been over this part, Leroy, back when I read you the first half of this story, the one I call THE DRIVE-IN, A B-MOVIE WITH BLOOD AND POPCORN. Yes, the one written on the Big Chief tablets. But to answer your question why . . . I don't know. It's like why do turds come in different shapes and colors. I can't answer that. It's one of life's big mysteries, and the comet is an even bigger one.

Here, listen. Do you remember those sayings I taught

51

you? The ones the Christians are fond of. Remember, we talked about Christians. Good? Now, those sayings. Let's use them to get things on the roll and because they're all-purpose. Repeat after me: THERE ARE SOME THINGS MAN WAS NOT MEANT TO KNOW, *and* I FEEL IT IN MY HEART. *Later I'll teach you about* Faith, *that way if you don't know how to explain something, say,* I've got faith. *That covers a lot of bases and cuts down on argument.*

What do you mean that doesn't work for you? Is this going to be like yesterday's conversation, Leroy? The one about Why Is There Air *and* Why Do Boys Have a Pecker and Girls Don't? *Good, because I'm not going to get into that. I've got a story written down here and it's the story I'm going to read. It's a good story and I've recorded it as best I can, and it's almost the truth. If you want to hear it, fine, if not, I'll read to myself. I do this for me, not you, so you want to hear the story you got to listen. What, Leroy?*

Uh huh, that's right. Why don't you go ahead and find your stick again and stir the shit pile. At least you were quiet. I wish I hadn't disturbed you.

Yeah, that's okay, use your finger. Let me get back to Grace—

Okay, maybe I don't remember what Grace said word for word, but this is pretty close. Trust me.

Food started running out at the concession, so we used Timothy's pocket knife to cut strips from the leather seat covers. The leather must have been coated with something (a dirt-resistant spray?), because it made us sick at first, though after a while we got used to it. When we still had Coke from the concession, we'd soak it in that and chew on it, maybe finish off with a few chocolate almonds. But when everything was gone at the concession we had to eat the strips straight out.

All around us people were losing it, going nuts for food, killing one another and eating one another. Sue Ellen wasn't doing so hot either. She seemed addled most of the time and kept insisting we take her home, that Mommy and Daddy would be worried. She said she didn't like the movies anymore. She missed her dog. She said lots of things.

I had to use my martial arts a few times to keep from being hurt by nuts who wanted me for either sex or food. We never got the situation clear; I pounded their heads briskly and they went away. But in time I got too weak for the martial arts, and a lot of the folks around us were too weak to do much of anything either. I guess you could say it was a kind of trade-off. I didn't feel so good, but the folks that might have done me, Timothy and Sue Ellen harm, weren't exactly up for the Boston Marathon either.

Then along came the Popcorn King.

Now he was one weird sonofabitch, looking back on it, but I'll tell you, when those two guys were fused together by the lightning and they had all those powers, tattoos coming to life and running around and the like, I wasn't even surprised.

Weird was the status quo, right?

What did surprise me was when he used those powers of his to supply us with popcorn and Coke, and he started talking that stuff about how he was our savior and that the movies were reality and murder and mayhem were okey-dokey and our salvation, and by the way, got any dead bodies, bring them on over to me and I'll eat them. You know the rap.

When he stopped giving out the popcorn and disappeared inside the concession stand for a time, like Jesus gone off into the wilderness, I'll tell you true, I was some depressed. It was back to eating seat covers.

When he finally did reappear, he no longer had popcorn to give us. Least not the real stuff. Now it was that substitute crap he was vomiting up. And that had bloodshot eyeballs on it.

Weirdness suddenly reidentified and redefined itself. I wasn't going to eat that junk, no way, no how. And neither was Timothy.

Sue Ellen ate it. There wasn't any way we could stop her from it. We tried at first, but she got away and got to it anyhow. She said it was sweet as candy and ran around inside your head like a hot lizard; said looking out of her eyes was like looking through a projector, like becoming the light and sound that shot out of the projector and hit the screen; like being everything fast-moving and bright that ever existed. Stuff like that, not twelve-year-old talk. She said when she looked at us she saw little screens on our faces instead of eyes and on the screens she could see little picture shows of our past, and I guess maybe she could, because she told us some things we hadn't told her about the two of us, like about the time we played doctor.

Mysterious stuff. Popcorn magic.

And in time the eyeball corn didn't seem so odd. So what, big deal, the popcorn had eyeballs and it came from the King who vomited it up? So what?

The idea of crunching down on those eyeballs wasn't so weird anymore. I thought maybe in texture it might be like damp Cracker Jack. Was it the vomit that made it sweet? Did lights and shadows and sounds run around in your head like a hot lizard, as Sue Ellen said? Was it really like that? Would I know new and wonderful things?

I looked around at the others. They were eating the corn, but they didn't seem to be cruising through life any better than I was. They were weak and sick and malicious, always hungry. They were dying same as me except they were hiding behind the veneer of the King's chemistry, mixing it with his jive religion, but they were going to die same as me.

Still, you can only hold out so long. Hunger is the biggest monkey ever made. It can make heroin addiction seem like a Coca-Cola habit.

Timothy caved in. He got tired of chewing seat covers and listening to his belly rumble. He went the way of Sue Ellen and ate the vomit corn. First time he had it he came back talking about the color of lies. His breath was sewerish and his eyes were dull; I wondered what movies were showing on the backs of them.

I used my martial arts to keep me away from the corn. I was too weak to practice it, but I did the movements in my head, tried to fill the hungry thoughts with visions of me nude and strong and practicing every technique I knew, fast and slow and medium.

It worked well, but not well enough. In time my belly started to win over, and I would have gone for the corn had the man not come along.

This is hard to talk about, but it seems to me, bad as this was, it was better than the corn. The corn would make me sing the King's song; I wasn't ready for the color of lies and movies on the backs of my eyes.

Okay, here goes. Straight plunge.

Timothy and Sue Ellen were just back from the concession, sitting in the car, eyes closed, seeing whatever it was the corn made them see, and I was sitting there thinking of stripping off another piece of seat cover to chew on. There wasn't much left and it made me ill to think about chewing on that nasty stuff, but what else was there to do? So I'm thinking about this, trying to get the will to do it, when this man staggered by on my side, put his hand against the door frame, said, "Shit, this ain't heartburn," and fell over.

I got out of the car and looked at him. He was about thirty with long, stringy, grayish hair and he was lying on his stomach with his head turned to one side, his eyes open. But he wasn't seeing much. He had been correct. It wasn't heartburn. He was as dead as a dodo's agenda.

Sue Ellen and Timothy got out of the car and came around and looked at him, then looked at each other, and finally me.

We didn't say a word. We got hold of him and put him in the backseat and Sue Ellen got back there with him, and Timothy and I got in the front.

Of course, I knew what we were doing. We were saving him for food. I hadn't been willing to eat popcorn with eyeballs on it, but somehow this was different. It would have been a shame to let him go to waste when we were starving. And if we didn't eat him, someone else was going to come along and drag him off for just that purpose.

Hell, it wasn't like we'd killed him.

I remember sitting there thinking about this, turning from time to time to look at the body on the backseat, and finding that each time I looked, Sue Ellen had removed yet another article of his clothing. When he was completely stripped, she called for Timothy's knife, and he gave it to her.

My next memory is of holding the corpse's still-warm liver in my hands and rubbing it into my face, then eating it. Strength flowed back into me immediately, and for some reason my legs began to jerk spasmodically and my knees hit the bottom of the dash and caused the glove box to knock open.

Timothy kept a little mirror in there, and it was at an angle, and by the light of the pulsating Orbit symbol, I could see myself. My face was stained a rust color from forehead to chin, and my eyes were little pits.

I looked at Timothy and Sue Ellen.

Timothy was chewing on a bone with a few chunks of meat on it. He had his eyes closed, and when he chewed he made little orgasmic noises deep in his throat.

Sue Ellen was on her hands and knees straddling the body, and she had half her head buried in an opening she had cut in the man's stomach. She was rooting around in there like a pig.

I opened the door and fell on the ground and threw up.

I don't think Timothy or Sue Ellen noticed. They were too busy with lunch.

I crawled under the Galaxy and tried to wipe the blood off my face with my forearms, then lay on my side with my knees pulled into my chest, and shook.

A young man so thin his pants flapped around his legs like flags on poles, came by, dropped to the ground, and made a meal of what I'd thrown up. His face was turned toward me as he lapped. When he saw me, he lapped faster. Maybe he thought I wanted it.

He finally staggered off. Where my vomit had been was a damp spot.

I rolled on my back and looked at the underside of the car and tried to think about nothing, but all I could see was that man gutted from throat to crotch and Sue Ellen with her head dipped into him. And lastly, my own face in that mirror, smeared with blood from hair to chin.

Bones were dropped out of the Galaxy's windows on the left side, and I turned my head and looked at them and tried to determine if they were rib, forearm, or leg bones. I couldn't make a decision.

As I watched, people came along and snatched up the bones and ran off with them.

I lay there for the longest time, feeling very sick to my stomach and my soul.

When I heard Timothy and Sue Ellen getting out of the Galaxy, I refused to watch their legs go by. I knew they were going to the concession to get their vomit corn from the King. I had decided I would starve to death before I did that.

I don't know how long this went on, my lying under the car hoping to starve. It could have been thirty minutes or it could have been days. But Timothy and Sue Ellen came and went several times and I always felt dizzy, as if I were in the middle of some huge platter that was being spun.

But my starvation plans weren't working out. The hunger had a mind of its own, and finally I crawled out from under the car and tried to stand up. But couldn't. I was too weak. I got hold of a door handle and pulled myself up and looked in the window at the body on the backseat.

There was hardly anything left of the man. Even his eyes and genitals had been eaten. Only his pelvis, ankles and feet had flesh on them, and it was turning black.

I felt hungry enough to bite the toes off his feet, one at a time, and would have tried, but about the time I started to go after him, the concession stand blew up.

4

That was us that did it, of course, and no use going into that again. Anyway, we smashed the concession, killed the King, and for our fine work, the crowd got hold of us and crucified us. But, I told you all about that too.

Summing up this part of Grace's story, she didn't see what happened to the concession, but when she turned around it was in shambles and on fire. Of course the movies from the concession were snuffed too, though the projector over in B section of the lot was still pumping. But the thing is, we killed the King.

Grace's dizziness subsided, and she managed to walk toward the flames. She saw what was happening to us, but later when she met us, she didn't remember our faces. The crowd was about to put fires under the crosses and cook us, and the comet came back. The black goo went away, and the drive-in folks were out of there.

Grace wanted to help get us down. Her dizziness had passed, and she tried to talk Timothy and Sue Ellen into helping, but they had come back to the car and they were ready to leave.

Anyway, Grace said—

* * *

I got the keys from Timothy and pulled the body out of the backseat. Doing that made me dizzy again, but I put a hand on the side of the car and stood that way until it passed.

I went around back to the trunk and opened it. I wanted to find something I could use as a tool to get those people down off those crosses, but there wasn't much there. A tire tool, a spare, and a bag full of golf clubs. I leaned down deeper, seeing if maybe there was something way in the back, and when I did, my head felt as if it were flying apart.

And as they say in the old detective movies, I fell into a deep, dark pit and it closed around me.

"I didn't mean to hit you that hard," Timothy said.

"Someone meant to," I said. "What did you use?"

"A golf club."

It was bright daylight and I was stretched out on the ground beside the Galaxy, which was parked on the grass next to the highway. I felt a little too warm.

Timothy helped me to a sitting position and gave me a piece of fruit. After what we'd been eating, it tasted like heaven. I began feeling better immediately. Which is not to say the golf-ball-size lump (which was appropriate) had gone away.

"I panicked," Timothy said. "I was afraid it would go back to how it was. I'm thinking better now that I've had some food."

I looked for Sue Ellen and spotted her sitting in the shade of a big tree, eating fruit. She was rocking a little and humming to herself.

"She's not doing so good," Timothy said.

He got an arm under me and helped me to my feet. I

looked down the highway and saw nothing but more highway bordered by jungle and topped by blue sky.

"I've got to go back to the Orbit," I said.

"I can't do that," Timothy said. "Neither can Sue Ellen."

"Just take me back. You don't have to go in."

"We've come a long ways since I hit you."

"You owe me, Timothy."

He drove me back and waited while I went inside the drive-in. I thought maybe I could find something in a car there to use as a tool to get those folks down, if they were still alive. But when I got inside, the crosses were down and they were gone.

I didn't stick around to look at the empty cars or the bones. I went outside to where the Galaxy was waiting, and we started on down the highway.

Okay, gang, I'll interrupt here to say that we stopped Grace's story and told her that Bob and me were two of the folks on the cross, and Crier was the one that got us down. And when we finished that, she picked up with her adventures.

But before we get to those, why don't we take a brief intermission. My tongue is getting tired.

INTERMISSION

Now, does everyone feel better?
Good. Let's continue then with Grace's story.

THIRD REEL

(Grace Tells of Tremendous Gas Mileage, Shit Town,
and Popalong Cassidy)

1

So we went on down the highway, traveling only a few miles a day, stopping to look around, relieve ourselves and search for fruit and berries.

I was amazed at the way the gas held out. It was like when we were in the drive-in and the electricity worked for no logical reason, and now here was the gas gauge showing us to be getting incredible mileage. It was going down all right, but slowly compared to the miles we were racking up.

Still, gas was going to be a problem eventually. But it was a problem that was solved when we came to a place with lots of cars pulled off the highway and parked along its edges and out in an area that had been partially cleaned by nature and partially by human beings.

A crude sign had been painted on a big, split limb and stuck up in the ground beside the road. It read:

S
H
I
T

T
O
W
N

People were living in their cars and crude huts. There was a river nearby and they were getting fish out of it. And, of course, there was abundant fruit.

You wouldn't call it a harmonious little town, but it seemed to be doing well enough, considering a canopy of doom hung over it; a canopy knitted stitch by stitch by dark experience.

We stayed on a while, living out of our car, watching the place try and become a real town.

One night this guy about my age got a rope from somewhere and went out to the edge of town and picked this big oak and threw the rope over a limb and fashioned a noose and hung himself.

Next morning he was dangling there, purple-faced, looking like some odd-shaped, overripe fruit about to drop from the vine. The log he had stood on and kicked away at the last moment was about six feet from where his feet dangled. I wondered if in his last painful moments he had looked down at the log with regret.

Timothy and I helped get him down and some others got rid of the body, and the next night, a girl of about twelve went out there and climbed up on the limb and put the rope around her neck and hung herself.

In the morning she was discovered. Sue Ellen went over to look at her. Neither Timothy nor I tried to stop her from seeing the body. She had seen much worse than that, and keeping her from it was akin to shutting the barn door after the stock have run off. Still, the way she looked at the dead girl's face made me shiver. You'd have thought she was gazing on the countenance of the Madonna.

No one cut the rope down. I think it was a way out everyone liked knowing was there, even if they never actually planned to use it.

New people joined the community regularly. They had all been down the road a piece and they had given up and turned back, coming rolling into Shit Town in cars propelled by little more than fumes. Or they walked in, weary and defeated.

I was still thinking about the end of the highway, so I talked to as many newcomers as I could. No one I spoke with had made it to the end. They said it got rougher and stranger as you went, and some of them felt certain the highway never ended.

The town grew and the rope became more popular. Sue Ellen spent a lot of time looking at it. I decided it was time to move on.

Timothy agreed. He spent his days gathering stones and taking them out to the middle of the highway and putting them on the fading yellow line and swatting them with a golf club. His strength, like mine, had come back, and he could knock them real far. He did that day in and day out until it was too dark to do it. He didn't talk much.

I talked to people in the town that had cars, asked if I could have their gas. A lot of them said they had gone all they intended to go, and they gave it to me. I managed to get a can and a hose. I siphoned gas from the cars into the can and transferred it to the Galaxy.

While I did this, Timothy golfed and Sue Ellen looked at the rope.

I put a can of gas in the trunk and some fruit too, then I got Timothy and Sue Ellen and drove us out of there. Timothy wasn't shit for driving anymore. He couldn't keep his mind on it, and the King's popcorn had done something to the both of them. They had flashbacks of a sort. Recited lines from the movies back at the Orbit. Sue Ellen could even do the nail gun noise from *The Toolbox Murders*.

Anyway, we drove on out of there, and I put the pedal to the metal and kept my eyes ever forward, searching for the end of the highway.

2

We went along quickly, stopping only to sleep and get fruit from the trunk of the car, but after a few days, things began to change.

It was getting along night when I first noticed it. As it grew darker the jungle grew thicker and great roots cracked the concrete and coiled onto the highway along with vines that twisted and knotted like threads in a complex tapestry.

When the Galaxy's tires went over the big roots, the shocks throbbed, and when they went over the larger vines, the vines exploded like garden hoses full of black water.

The sun, like a head full of fire, nodded out below the pinprick of the highway's horizon, and the moon rose up in the same spot like a mean little kid giving us a bent-over view of a pockmarked ass.

I turned on the lights and the trees on either side of the highway leaned forward and touched overhead making a tunnel of foliage down which the Galaxy was shooting like a bullet out of a gun barrel.

The wind picked up and leaves churned across the road and popcorn bags and soft drink cups and candy wrappers joined them and made a little twister that fell over the windshield of the Galaxy like an avalanche. I beat the refuse away with the wipers and went though another twister of the stuff, and yet another, each gaining strength and causing the car to shake violently.

I thought I could see drive-in screens, or fragments of old drive-ins, on either side of the road, but I couldn't be sure because of the shadows.

Something came blowing toward me and plastered to the windshield and there was no way I could make out for sure what it was before it blew away, but it looked like a movie poster, one of those garish ones you see in the horror movies.

I glanced at Timothy, but he had passed out some time back and was leaning against the door, snoring softly. Sue Ellen was stretched out on the backseat asleep.

Goose bumps went up my back, but I didn't slow down and I didn't pull over. I didn't know what I'd find out there if I pulled over, and the idea of slowing down bothered me, especially now that the shadows were growing thicker and looking funny, and I use the word funny in the loosest sense, because I wasn't laughing about anything. I wasn't even cracking a smile.

The shadows fluttered and rolled across the road like tumbleweeds and hit the car with a sound like wet blankets. They were very odd shadows indeed. Shadows of trees and leaves and men and women and giant apes and dinosaurs and flying things bigger than a double-decker bus.

I couldn't see the source of any of the shadows, but I had a feeling if they had a source, they lived lives contrary to the movements of their origins.

I thought I saw movements in my mirror, faces, reflections of things in windows, thought I heard whispers, laughs and sighs.

Then it started to get really bad out there. The wind

picked up and gathered in the shadows, the popcorn bags, candy wrappers, cups, and posters (I was sure now), all this stuff, and it began to hit the Galaxy and whirl about it and the wind sucked at the car and lifted it up and dropped it down, lifted it up and dropped it down, and once when it went down, the back right tire went with a noise like a six-gun shot.

The car swerved and I tried to turn in the direction of the skid like the handbook says, but the skid said "Fuck You," and the shadows sacked up the car and took away the light.

Round and round the Galaxy went, over and over. Timothy flew into me and we banged heads and the darkness outside became the darkness in me.

3

I woke up and found that the car had righted itself and that I was lying on the front seat alone. The door on the passenger side was open.

I sat up and clung to the back of the seat until I felt focused. I could see Sue Ellen's shape in the back, draped partially on the floorboard and partially on the seat. I reached back and touched her and she moaned and sat up slowly and held the side of her jaw.

"You okay?" I asked.

"The movie over yet?" she asked.

"Not yet," I said. I took her hand gently from her face and saw a thin cut running from the corner of her mouth to her chin, a scratch really. She didn't seem to be in any real pain.

"Wait here, okay?"

"You going to the concession stand?"

"I'll be right back."

"Where's Timmy?"

"I'm going to get him."

"Have him bring me a large popcorn, will you?"

I couldn't tell if the wreck had banged her around and thrown off her time frame, or if she was having another of those pop-backs. Maybe she was seeing a movie through the windshield of the car.

The wind was still high when I got out of the car, but not as bad as before. I held on to the door handle for a moment, edged my way to the rear of the car. The trunk was open and the keys were in the trunk lid. Timothy had gotten the keys and gotten back here. Maybe he wanted some of the fruit.

I got the keys and put them in my pants pocket and saw that his golf bag had been pulled from under all the fruit. It was sticking out of the back of the car by a foot. I knew then that he had gotten one of his golf clubs. If Sue Ellen was still at the drive-in watching movies, maybe Timothy thought he was participating in the Bob Hope Open, or whatever that golf thing is called.

There was mashed fruit all over the place and the gas can was banged up, but not open. I set it up and got a piece of fruit and ate a few bites out of it, and started looking for Timothy.

The wind passed on by, and the last of it let popcorn bags and debris flutter onto the car and ground. Plastered across the rear of the windshield was a poster. The moon was brighter, now that the shadows had fled, and I could read the printing on the poster. *Texas Chainsaw Massacre.* The words looked as if they had been written in blood.

Out in the trees I could see big hunks of whiteness. I decided they were fragments of drive-in screens—chunks of white painted wood.

Draped between the trees like Christmas decorations were lengths of film, the moonlight sticking through the sprocket holes like long, bright needles, and a sort of mist swirling about the film itself.

I didn't see any videotapes, and I didn't see Timothy. I went around the car a couple of times, examining it.

Except for a lot of bumps and a hairline crack in the windshield, it looked all right. It was no more than ten feet from the highway, and the ground between it and the highway looked firm enough to drive on.

I wanted to look for Timothy, but I didn't know if we might need the car in a hurry, and I wanted to be ready. I dug around under the fruit and the golf bag and got out the tire iron and the spare.

The jacking up and the tire changing went pretty quick, and I rolled the old tire off beside the road, tossed the tire tool in the back and closed the trunk.

I started looking for Timothy.

Out to the right there was a trail. Maybe dinosaurs had made it. Maybe cars had made it. There was no rhyme or reason to this place.

I went down the trail calling for Timothy. As I went the wind picked up again and it started to rain and lightning began to crackle in the heavens. Still, the moon held bright.

Something moved in the jungle, and I found a good-size stick and carried it with me. Martial arts or not, another equalizer never hurts. Course, if it was a Tyrannosaurus Rex, something like that, it would eat me and pick its teeth with my stick.

As I went along, the trail widened. I went over a little rise and down into a clearing. There was a lot of grass and there were posts for drive-in speakers, and a few of them still had speakers on them. There were rusted cars dotted about.

At the back, almost integrated into the jungle, was a drive-in screen. It was split open in spots and limbs poked through the splits and twisted upwards and spread out in leaf-covered branches that looked like bony fingers from which dangled tufts of dark flesh.

About ten yards in front of the screen, golf club in hand, on the tail end of a classic swing, was Timothy.

I stood and watched a while. He was golfing up dirt and leaves.

I called to him. He looked up, went back to golfing. I walked over and waited until he finished a swing, then I stepped in and took hold of his elbow.

"This is a tough course," he said.

"You can say that again."

"I don't think I'm doing too well."

"You're doing fine. That was the last hole."

"Yeah. How'd I do?"

"You beat the competition hands down. Come along, Sue Ellen is waiting for us."

I led him along and the wind picked up and the trash twisters coiled at our feet.

4

Serious rain.

Serious wind.

Serious lightning.

Serious lost.

"Where the hell are we?" Timothy asked.

"Well, Toto, I don't think we're in Kansas anymore."

"Kansas? We've been in Kansas? Who's Toto?"

"Just close your little mouth and walk."

Sometimes it doesn't pay to read or watch old movies. No one knows what you're talking about.

"Goddamn," Timothy said. "This is a weird course. What's that?"

It was shadows. They had collected in our path. On either side of us the trees whipped their heads up and down like drunk women with the dry heaves.

I threw my stick at the shadows and the stick went into them and was not seen again. The shadows flowed over us with a howl of the wind and they felt like wet felt where they touched us. But there was nothing more to them. They went through us, and I turned to watch them blow on down the trail like ink-stained ghosts.

The trail disappeared. It was as if the trees had pulled

up by the roots and repositioned themselves. Nothing was familiar. Strips of film dropped down from the branches and clung to us, and when I tore them off they ripped my flesh.

Timothy swatted at them with his golf club. The film wound itself around the club and jerked it away from him. Last sight of it was a silver wink in the moonlight as it disappeared into the rustling leaves of a dark, gnarled tree.

I grabbed hold of his wrist and tugged him. We went between trees and shrubs, wherever there was a space. Film ran along the ground and dropped out of the trees and tried to grab us.

Lightning flashed. I got a glimpse of the highway through the trees. Not much farther.

Timothy was pulled from me. I turned. The film had him by the feet and more of it had dropped down from the trees and coiled around his arms and pulled them up. A thin strip of it was twisting around his leg and working up his body. By the time I reached him, the end of it was tight around his neck.

I tried to pull it off of him, but more of it came up from the forest floor and snapped around me like the business end of a whip. Then my feet were held and my arms went up and more of it wrapped around my body. Where it touched my bare skin I could feel a sensation like dozens of tiny needles.

From where I stood, immobile, I could see a clear spot in the trees, and when the lightning flashed, I saw the highway, and out there on the highway was a black wrecker with its light on. A man was standing by the wrecker looking at the jungle and the wrecker door was open and I could see a naked butt rising and falling, and there was something between the butt and the seat, white-legged

and thrashing, and I knew instantly that it was poor Sue
Ellen.

And I knew too that the same lightning that had
flashed and allowed me to see the man by the wrecker had
allowed him to see me.

5

A flashlight bounced like a great firefly toward us. When the light reached the edge of the jungle I could see the outline of a big, broad-shouldered man and the outline of another behind him. Their shadows leaned together behind them like two happy thugs. When the men moved, the shadows moved of their own accord.

As they entered into the jungle the film crept out and grabbed at them and the biggest of the two men yelled, "Edit," and produced some large scissors and snipped at the film. The man behind him did the same with a smaller pair.

They clipped their way through, and one came up to me, the other to Timothy.

The one with the big scissors and the flashlight was the one in front of me. He put the light in my face and said, "How would you like to be cast in the part of prime pussy?"

Film crawled on his legs and he bent casually and clipped it. "Damn stuff," he said.

"This one looks like a dumb asshole," said the other.

Some of the old Timothy came back, and it couldn't have been a worse time. Timothy said, "Fuck you."

The man hit Timothy in the side of the head with the little scissors. Timothy nodded forward, made no further sounds.

The little scissors went to work on the film that held Timothy, and when it was snipped, Timothy fell down. The man picked him up and tossed him over his shoulder and headed toward the highway, kicking at the film as he went. Once he squatted with Timothy balanced on his shoulder, and used the scissors on a swathe of film.

"Snip, snip, snip, you little motherfuckers," he said. Then he and Timothy were out of the jungle, being pursued by both men's shadows; they moved out into the brighter moonlight which had replaced the dark and the lightning. Out on the highway the wind made little plumes of trash jig all around the wrecker.

The man in front of me cut a coil of film from around my neck and snipped an even smaller piece from that, held it three feet from me. It dripped blood.

"They're like leeches. They show best when they've eaten." He put the flashlight against the strip from behind and two hands holding a chainsaw came out on my side and ballooned to full size and the chainsaw buzzed and the hands shoved it at my face.

He turned out the light just in time. The buzz of the saw died, and where the hands and saw had been, were drops of falling blood. I felt them hit my shoe.

The man cocked the flashlight and said, "Good night, moon," and he hit me.

I was still bound when I awoke, but I was no longer in the jungle. I was tied to the wrecker, facing out. The wrecker was off the highway and a tarp had been stretched over it and the end visible to me was stretched down tight with stakes, and the center of it was poked up high with an antenna stalk that bloomed into a clutch of silver quills at the top.

It was warm under the tarp, and the warmth came

from fires built in the husks of a dozen television sets. Rain pounded the tarp and scratched at it like harpy claws. Some of it came through the holes in the tarp and hissed in the fire and hit my face and ran down it like tears. The televisions gave off greasy smoke and it fouled the air and made me woozy.

The side of my head hurt. It should. I had been knocked on it enough. But considering all that, I was lucky. My dad always said I had a hard head. On the other hand, I have dizzy spells from time to time even now. My vision gets screwy.

But as I was saying. My head hurt. Where the film touched me stung.

To the rear of the tarp, squatting in a semicircle, facing me, were four men. They were all dressed in ragged clothes and jeans. They were close-shaved and had bushy flattops that looked as if they had been cut with dull knives. They looked strong and well fed, or maybe just fed. Two of them were the men who had taken Timothy and me out of the jungle.

Behind them on the tarp were their shadows. The shadows were moving in defiance of the motionless posture of the men and the flickerings of the firelight.

I looked to the right of me and saw Timothy. He was tied to the wrecker by blue and red electrical wire. I assumed the same thing held me. Where the man had hit him with the scissors his skull had cracked open and a coil of his brain was leaking out like congealed oatmeal escaping from a crack in a bowl. Suddenly it was very hot. I thought I was going to faint. The wire was the only thing holding me up; there were no usable muscles left in me.

I took a deep breath and pulled some strength back into me from somewhere and looked to my left and saw Sue Ellen. She was tied to the wrecker by wire too. She had her clothes on now. Both her eyes had been blacked and her bottom lip was puffed. The front of her pants was dark with blood. She had her eyes open and she was looking straight ahead, but she wasn't seeing what was there. She was tuned in to something else. Maybe a flashback of one of the movies she liked. I hoped so. This little scenario was certainly a stinker.

Then the four in the back rose and their shadows went still and rigid. They were staring at me, or so I thought at first, but realized that they were in fact staring at something behind me. I could sense the presence of that something, and I heard movement on the wrecker and I could hear a sound like breathing through a bad drive-in speaker, puff and crackle, puff and crackle.

Goose bumps rose along my arms and ripped up my back and down my spine, felt as big as black berries. They were even on the backs of my calves. Then the sensation passed and the wrecker creaked and I knew that whatever had been behind me had moved.

I watched the heads of the men in back turn; watched the heads of their shadows turn. The fires flickered and popped when the cold rain came through the holes in the tarp and went into them and was turned to steam.

There was movement on the wrecker again, then whatever it was jumped to the ground between Sue Ellen and myself, and I got my first look at the thing I would come to know as Popalong Cassidy.

6

Leave It to Beaver was playing on his face and his face was a sixteen-inch screen with one of those old-fashioned glow lights trimmed around it, and this was all encased in a cheap brown wooden case. The character on the screen, Ward Cleaver, closed a door and said, "Honey, I'm home," and this was all faint, this dialogue, because there was lots of static right then. And behind all this, in the depths of that tube-face, I could see two red glows that might have been little tubes or eyes.

The television set was wearing a tall, black hat. There was a white scarf around a very human neck, and the rest of the figure was human too, and it was dressed all in black, drugstore-cowboy attire. The pants were stuffed into some tall, black boots and there was a black glove on either hand. He wore a black gun belt with some metal studs on it and there was a holster on each hip and in the holsters were pearl-handled, silver-tooled revolvers.

Television Face came and stood in front of me, and I saw below his screen, on the cheap wooden frame, two rows of knobs and dials. They divided suddenly so that they looked like top and bottom teeth, which in a way they were.

The thing was smiling. The wood was not wood.

A tongue made of tangled blue and red wires licked from left to right and disappeared. In its place came a voice full of static and high of tone. "Hi. My name is Popalong Cassidy, and I bet you think we are mean."

The hat lifted and I saw a set of rabbit ear antennas were responsible. They wiggled out cautiously, as if testing the air for radiation. The hat tipped way back but didn't fall off; it fit there like a flap of skin.

A blue arc jumped from the tip of one ear to the other and the arc rode down the middle space between the ears, then back up. *Leave It to Beaver* went away and on the screen there was a dumpy, ugly man down on one knee next to a Highway Patrol car. The car door was open and the man reached inside and took a microphone from off the dash and pulled it out until the wire was stretched. He said something into the microphone I didn't catch, ended it with "Ten-four." I realized then that he was down like that because on the other side of his car, way off the highway, hid out there in the brush-covered hills, there was supposed to be a bad guy with a gun.

I recognized the television series. It was an old black-and-white one I had watched on occasion. It was called *Highway Patrol* and starred Broderick Crawford.

I didn't get to find out if Crawford went after the culprit in the brush or not, because Popalong darkened his face except for a little yellow dot in the center, and that grew rapidly smaller until it too was gone. The rabbit ears slid back into the set and the hat fell back into place.

"It's okay if you think we're mean, you know. I don't mind." And with that Popalong backed away from me until he was up against the big antenna that punched up the middle of the tarp. There was a bar that ran through the bottom of the antenna, about four inches off the ground, and Popalong back-stepped onto that and reached his arms up and draped them through the antenna rods, hung his head to the side and let his body droop. Presto, a media Christ.

The rain plummeted the tarp and slipped through the holes and sizzled in the popping fires. Nobody said a thing or moved a muscle.

After a while, one of the men got up and raced to the wrecker and climbed on it. When he jumped off he had a big load of magazines under each arm. He went from TV to TV and put magazines into their blazes. I saw the covers of some of the magazines before the flames devoured them. *TV Guide, People, Tiger Beat, Screen Gems,* all of them decorated with the faces of movie stars and fading celebrities. I thought: Where in hell did that stuff come from?

When the fires were really popping and the air was tinged with smoke, the man darted back to his place with the others, and Popalong lifted his head and looked at me and turned his face on. A test pattern filled it. The dials below the screen split apart again and the tongue of tangled wire presented itself briefly and disappeared. "Don't think there's any hatred in my heart for you or anyone," Popalong said. "My heart has no room for that. It's full of electro-magnetic waves and they jump about like frogs."

He got down off the antenna and came over and bent forward and looked at me, as if hoping to find something reflected in my eyes. The rabbit ears poked out from under the hat and touched my hair and I felt a faint electric sizzle ride the circumference of my skull. "You have no shadow, you know. It's because you haven't learned to belong. That's what I think. I think when you belong here you have a shadow. I think you earn it. You haven't earned anything. When you're like us you'll have a shadow, a familiar made up of the absence of light.

"Pay attention. Keep sharp. I jump around a lot, It's

the sign of a good mind. I'm trying to tell you there's a confusion about good and evil. We worry about which is which way too much. Let me just say that good is too easy. It requires nothing. No real commitment. You can't get the real good out of goodness until you know darkness. Death. Pain. These are instructive tools. Or as Dr. Frankenstein said in *Andy Warhol's Frankenstein*, 'To know death, you have to fuck life in the gall bladder.'

"I know this now, but all my life I have been looking for this truth and it's been under my nose all the time. The images taught me where it was at. There are good images and there are bad images, but the bad images make the best show, so I've opted for the bad images. I praise the Orbit for leading me to the truth. I praise the night I went. The Popcorn King was right. Movies are reality and everything else is fraud. But the King was not the Messiah, as I thought. He was John the Baptist. I'm the Messiah. I was given powers and position by the Producer and the Great Director, and they wanted a sci-fi horror picture. We're number two of a double feature.

"Why me, you ask? Because I have seen more hours of television than anyone. I can quote commercials by heart. I know the name of the Green Hornet's secret identity, the name of the sleek, black car he drives. I know the name of Sky King's niece and what Batman eats for breakfast. Everything that is important is in this square head.

"Let me tell you too, I was made for it. I'm a preacher's son. I grew up with fire and brimstone and channel nine, the only channel we could get at that time.

"My father spoke savagely to us from the pulpit and every Sunday afternoon after church he beat my mother with his thick belt, then came downstairs and beat me too. I never ran. I took it. He would beat me until his arm got tired, then he would switch arms and wear down. He left welts on my ass.

"When he was finished, he would become remorseful and read the Bible to me and pray. Then he would tell me to turn on my television set and watch it. That I was redeemed. That the sin was cast out of me by pain.

"My mother went away when I was eleven. I thought about her a few days after she was gone, but I never missed her. She had been nothing more than someone around the house, going this way and that in a plaid housecoat and slippers with the backs broken down. She ate a lot of sweets and drank lots of coffee and sipped Nervine that she poured from a bottle into a great big spoon. She seldom spoke to me and never fixed meals. I took care of myself. I grew up on Cokes and Twinkies. The characters on TV spoke to me in her place.

"When I graduated, passed more out of courtesy than for any other reason, my father took his belt to me and beat me until I couldn't get off my knees. He gave me a new Sylvania set and told me to be gone by morning and to never come back. He had taken care of my raising until I was a man, and now I was a man, and to go.

"I went. I couldn't get a good job. The people out there were cruel. Unlike TV, they expected things of you. They wanted college educations. I wanted a satellite dish and more channels. The chance to see time and again *Apocalypse Now, Taxi Driver, The Andy Griffith Show*. It really didn't matter. Just images. My images. Part of my holy communion. Kurtz and Opie, Leatherface and Lassie, side by side.

"I ended up working at a filling station. I could never get the work straight. I mostly put nozzles in gas tanks and dreamed of *Gilligan's Island* and a trip on *The Love Boat*, of chain-sawing pretty people and stripping their flesh so that I could wear it, jacking off in a gutted corpse. I missed my father's belt. Gasoline ran over my shoes."

As he talked, silent scenes from films and TV shows and commercials ran across his screen like track stars. I couldn't take my eyes off of them. Something about them tugged at me. I felt drunk. I wanted Popalong to turn his face off and shut up. I wanted a hot bath and a good meal and a hot fuck. I wanted to be home in Nacogdoches, tooling down Main Street with the car windows down and a hot wind in my face, looking to see what historical house or building they would tear down next.

But what I got was more of Popalong.

7

But the boss kept me working even if I wasn't any good. It wasn't a place that got much business and nobody else wanted to work there because the pay was cheap. Lucky for the boss, I didn't need much and no one else would have me. He let me watch television there at the station between cars. I was between cars a lot.

The money I made kept me in Twinkies and Cokes, *TV Guide* and the cable. I saved up and bought a VCR. I bought a belt like my father used to beat me. I was cozy. I lived in a one-room, walk-up apartment that smelled like the winos in the doorways below. I often saw them when I was walking to work, shuffling ahead of me in search of a bottle. For some reason they made me think of Henry Fonda in *The Grapes of Wrath*.

At night I would take the belt like my father's and slap my naked back with it. I did this while I watched tapes of Hopalong Cassidy reruns. Hopalong had a face like my father's. Watching him made the beltings work all the better. I slapped myself until I bled. I tore pages from the *TV Guide* and stuck them to my back to stop the blood. Sometimes there were not enough pages.

When I finished, I would put the videotape of *The Bible* into the VCR and watch a few minutes of that while I knelt and held the box the tape had come out of. I prayed there would be no electrical blackouts while I was watching a movie. I prayed my television would not wear out until I could afford a big-screen TV. I prayed I would someday have a place of my own away from the noise of the winos, a place where I could have a satellite dish and fill my head with channels. I wondered who I was praying to.

So it went until a week before Halloween. I was on my way home from work, eager to get my belt and put in the Hopalong tape, and what do I see in the window of the costume shop between Sylvester the Cat and a pirate outfit, but a Hopalong Cassidy costume. I felt weak in the knees.

I went in there and blew all the money I had. I knew I would have to buy some cheap brand of soft drink and some sort of pastry that wouldn't match Twinkies, but I had my Hopalong suit, complete with hat and boots and holsters, though the guns in it were cap pistols.

When I got home I put the outfit on and looked in the mirror. I was disappointed. My shoulders were not as broad as Hoppy's and my face was nothing to look at. I didn't look like my father who looked like Hoppy. I looked like a weasel staring out of the woods.

I took off the suit and hung it in the closet and put the boots below and the hat on a shelf above. I discovered if I left the closet door cracked and turned on the end table light, or if the moonlight came through the window just right, it looked like Hoppy was standing in there, hiding, waiting to come out and beat me with a belt or shoot me with his pistols.

I liked that. The suit was not a total loss.

Then about Christmastime I saw this special on random killers. I noted that most of them had sad little faces

like mine. But here they were with their sad little faces
going out to millions while I lay in bed holding my dick.
They had done things like pump hot lead into warm bodies,
and all I could do was shoot a pathetic wet bullet onto my
sheets. What they had done brought camera crews out, and
they got their pictures taken. Got seen by millions. Got to
be stars. What I had was more laundry.

But when the special was over, I knew what I wanted
to do.

I had to save my money again, and this meant I didn't
eat very much, but I never really cared that much for eating
anyway. The more I thought about what I wanted to do, the
more excited I got, and the more I took the belt to myself.
When I showered it looked as if red paint were running
down the drain.

I took to wearing the Hopalong outfit. I didn't look any
better in it, but I didn't care anymore. I knew what I
wanted now, and knowing made me feel better about
myself.

First I bought a car from my boss for three hundred
dollars. A white Ford Fairlane. I was not a good driver, but
I knew how. I could get from one place to the next if I could
get my mind off television. I tried to pretend that I was part
of a television show like *Miami Vice*, and I was patrolling
the streets for crime. I drove every day so I could get better
at it, but I never learned to like it.

Then I saved up enough to get the rifle. A Winchester
with an old-fashioned lever. I had it replaced with a loop
cock like the one John Wayne had in *Stagecoach*. It was no
big problem to get the rifle. I merely had to sign some
papers. It didn't matter to me that later they would be able
to trace it. I wanted them to.

By the time the summer came around I was able to buy
two pearl-handled, silver-tooled pistols and enough ammu-

nition for them and the Winchester. Again, I merely had to sign some papers.

I went home and took the cap guns out of the holsters and put in the real .45's after I loaded them. I loaded the Winchester and put it in the closet. I watched a video of *The Wild Bunch*.

Next afternoon after work, I put the rifle in the trunk of my car and went back in and put the Hopalong outfit and gun belt on. The real guns weighed more than the cap pistols, but I liked their weight. It was like waking up and having muscles.

When I went out to the car the second time, a wino saw me. He said, "Man, who you supposed to be, Hopalong Cassidy?"

"That's right," I said, and pulled one of the .45s and shot at him. I missed him by a mile. The bullet went past him and smacked into the doorway of the apartment house. The wino ran around the corner, and I shot at him again. This shot wasn't any better. He got away. My marksmanship worried me some.

I drove out of town, and by the time I got to the overpass, it was starting to get dark. I pulled over next to the concrete wall and unlocked the trunk and got the rifle. It was dark now. I could see the lights of the cars, but to see who was in them I had to let them get pretty close to the overpass so the lights there would shine down on them and give me a look.

I watched a few go by before I shot at anybody. Guess I was getting the feel of things.

I picked one out and aimed between the headlights, then lifted the rifle barrel above that so I could center on the windshield, then I moved the barrel to the driver's position and pulled the trigger.

First time didn't work because I had the safety on. The car went beneath the underpass and on.

I took off the safety and waited for another car, remembered to cock the lever and jack a shell into the chamber. I felt like Lucas McCain, the Rifleman.

Next car that came I shot at, and I don't know if I hit anyone or not, but it veered off the road, then back on, and went under the overpass and kept going, very fast. Next car I hit someone because it went off the road and through a barbed wire fence right before it reached the underpass. I saw a man stumble out of it and fall down in the pasture and get up. I took a couple of shots at him, and I guess I finally hit him because he fell down and didn't get up. I shot once more in his direction, then went back to watching cars.

A station wagon was next, and I put a shot into it and it ran into the side of the overpass and a woman opened the door part of the way and fell out. The lights from the overpass were bright on the windshield in the car, and I could see a child in a baby seat on the passenger's side. I could even hear it crying.

I leveled the rifle and fired until I finally hit it and it shut up. I figured I had done enough then. I was a celebrity, though no one knew it yet. I could just imagine being apprehended and handcuffed and the television cameras coming out and taking my picture in my Hopalong outfit, and then taking pictures of my pistols and my loop-cock Winchester. I hoped they'd let me see myself on television in the jail. But just knowing I was going to be there was a great thrill. I was, for the first time in my life, somebody.

At first I thought I should turn myself in, but this seemed too easy. I would let them come for me. I might take a few shots at them, then, if they fired back, I would toss out my weapons and say I quit; I had watched that sort

of thing on television more than once. They didn't kill you
if you quit. After I got on television, I didn't care what they
did with me.

I put the rifle in the trunk and drove away. I drove
until I came to a little serve-yourself gas station and
grocery. I was very hungry and I needed gas.

I went in there and got a Coke and a Twinkie and the
girl behind the counter stared at me. I liked that. I felt like
a movie star. "Who are you supposed to be?" she said.

"Hopalong Cassidy," I said, and pulled out my pistol
and reached across the counter and put it next to her nose
and fired just as she screamed. Blood went all over the cash
register. I went around and opened it and got some of the
money just to have something to do, got my Coke and
Twinkie and started to leave.

A man in a big black wrecker drove up then, and he
walked inside just as I was about to go out. He looked at me
and I saw his head jerk a little. He knew something wasn't
right. I pulled the revolver and shot him in the chest and he
went back against the glass door, hitting it so hard it
cracked. It swung open and he fell out on the ground. I
bent over him and shot him twice in the head.

Something about the wrecker appealed to me. I put
my Coke and Twinkie in the wrecker's seat and got my rifle
out of the Fairlane and put it in the floorboard of the
wrecker. I had some trouble driving the wrecker at first,
but I knew how. I had learned how to drive a lot of things
at the station so I could put them in stalls to have flats and
oil changed.

I drove along not thinking about much, and I saw the
Orbit drive-in. I couldn't pass that up. I had been away
from a screen too long and had begun to feel unreal. I drove
in there and watched the movies and waited to be arrested.
I thought I might not even wait. I thought I could get my

rifle and go behind one of the screens and poke a hole in it and start shooting at people in their cars like the guy did in *Targets*. Maybe Boris Karloff would show up to stop me. I would have liked that.

But before I could do anything the comet came and trapped us all in the drive-in. I wasn't going to be arrested. I wasn't going to be on TV. It was depressing at first, until I realized an incredible truth. I was living a movie. This wasn't like working at the filling station. This wasn't like walking home and seeing the winos. This was even better than watching television. It was like when I was shooting from the top of the underpass, only more so. This was constant, and everyone had to be involved, like it or not. The movie owned us all and you couldn't change channels or turn it off. Here was a movie with blood and guts and a wild monster, the Popcorn King. He was wonderful. He preached violence and religion. If he could have gotten wrestling into his talks he would have covered the three manias of television. I loved him. I wanted him to beat me with a belt. I quit wearing the Hopalong outfit. I stripped off and went around naked like a lot of the others. I was not ashamed of my body now. Everyone looked awful. The comet and the Popcorn King had made us all alike. My constant fear was a happy ending, which meant, of course, everyone would go back to what they were before. And for me, that wouldn't have been much.

But things did not last. The comet came back. I put my Hopalong outfit on and drove out of the drive-in behind the others. I figured the old world would be out there and the only thing I could think of that was positive about that was that I would eventually be arrested and my picture would be on TV, and I would be recorded on video for all time. I figured this would be even more likely if I wore the Hopalong outfit.

But the old world wasn't out there. There was this world. This double feature.

I became determined to drive to the end of the highway. Things got weirder as I drove along, and I wanted to see just how weird they would get. I wanted to be part of the weird.

Once, when I stopped to find fruit, I saw a crowbar lying on the bed of the wrecker, and I got it and used it to break the padlock off the big metal box welded below the back window. Inside was a tarp, flares, knives, electrical wire, miscellaneous items. I knew these would come in handy later.

The gas in the wrecker lasted a long time, and when I got to this place with the film draped in the trees, I knew I was on the right track.

I pushed on. I felt like Humphrey Bogart in *They Drive by Night*.

Though the shadows and the storms and the crawling film persisted, I began to see new things. Solid things. Munchkins from *The Wizard of Oz*, for example. I never saw a live one, just dead ones. They were lying beside the highway or in it, obviously having been hit by cars. They were smashed and/or bloated. Their little caps lay beside them like markers. I passed one that someone had propped up with a stick. They also had a stick down one of his sleeves and had rigged it so his arm stuck straight out; he looked as if he were thumbing a ride.

I passed cars beside the road. Empty. Came to one where a body was wrapped like a mummy in film; the film was pulsing like a tumor.

Cars passed me on their way back. None of the drivers waved.

Beside the road I saw what looked like a collapsed

water tower, but it was one of the Martian stalking machines from *War of the Worlds*. A squidlike creature was dangling out of an opening in the top of the machine, limp as spaghetti.

When the storms came now, they were more violent than ever. The blue lightning flashed through the films and the images on the films were cast onto the ground and into the trees and onto the wrecker. They lived and breathed during those brief moments of lightning.

The wrecker was rigged with an auxiliary tank, and I switched that on and kept at it. I finally had to stop and use the hose from the box on the wrecker bed to siphon gas from a couple of dead cars, which turned out to be the last ones I saw on the highway. What gas I got from them you could have put in a paper cup. But it was gas that got me to the end of the highway.

I got closer looks at the Munchkins. They were solid all right, but they weren't real after all. They were elaborate dummies. As I went, there were more of these, and not all of them were Munchkins. They were the sort of dummies they used to use a lot in old movies, when they wanted to have a body tumble over Niagara Falls for instance. I stopped in the daylight and looked at the Martian machines. Cheap wood painted silver. The Martians were rubber octopuses.

I liked that.

Finally I came to the end of the highway.

And there was the Orbit.

It was different in many ways, but it was the Orbit. The highway was a snake biting its tail.

Amid the wreckage that had been made by the fools who killed the Popcorn King were strips of film, more dummies, props of all kinds, lobby cards, TV sets and fragments of antennas. In several spots there were piles of

TV sets; piles that made pyramids that tipped through a continuous bank of dark clouds.

At night there were really violent storms. Worse yet. The wind blew popcorn bags and movie posters and soft drinks and movie magazines against the wrecker with a sound like wet towels popping.

When it rained, it rained chocolate almonds and popcorn and soft drinks—every kind imaginable: cherry, orange, Coke, Dr Pepper, Pepsi. I recognized the taste of these and more by drinking from puddles in the blacktop. Later I sat cups out at night and in the morning I drank from these, picked up chocolate almonds and popcorn and the occasional unwrapped Snickers for my breakfast. I confess, I longed for Twinkies.

I learned that the busted television sets grew up from the ground like sacrificial potatoes. Once birthed, the ground healed up behind them like a sore.

I checked out the concession over in Lot B, but though it was intact, it was a shambles inside; there wasn't anything of use in there. The projectors looked okay, but unlike when the Orbit was in that black stuff, they didn't work without electricity. It was a depressing discovery. All those films and no way to show them.

The lightning gave me glimpses of films, because of the way it made images jump, but it was really more of a tease than anything else. What I would have given even for a complete dog food commercial.

I picked magazines—*Screen Gems*, *TV Guide*, and the like—off the windshields of the cars and off the ground, and spent my days shaking the soft drinks out of their pages and reading them carefully. It was okay at first, but a lot of the magazines were the same. I began to get bored. This place was certainly like a movie set, but it wasn't as satisfying as before, not the way it had been when it was at the other end of the highway. Then it had been more than a set. It had been a movie that I was part of. There was action and drama and comedy, and now there was just me. I didn't care much for me.

I decided to climb one of the pyramids and go up into the constant cloud bank. I doubted it was high enough for me to need an oxygen mask up there, and then again, I didn't really care. I wanted to see where all the chocolate almonds and soft drinks came from, and it was something to do that was like being in a movie.

I started up by sticking my feet into the busted faces of the sets, clutching them like lovers. After a time I realized the pyramid was much higher than I thought. I began to get frightened. I was reminded of the movie *The Bible* and the scene concerning the Tower of Babel. Was I defying the gods? Or was it a test?

Once again, I decided it didn't matter. I was living a movie and that was what counted. I would rather die as part of a movie than live as part of the normal world.

When night set in with its storms of papers and its rains of soft drinks, chocolate almonds, and popcorn, I was not even halfway up. I found a twenty-three-inch television with the tube busted out and I crawled into the opening and pushed out the back and found myself in a den of sets and movie magazines. It looked like someone or something had been living in there at one time. I crawled back through some more sets and found a comfortable spot with plenty of room and stretched out on top of some magazines and tried to pull a few over me. I lay there pretending I was Stewart Granger and I was trapped in King Solomon's mines.

When I awoke the next morning, I felt awful. I let down my pants and took a shit, got out of there and started climbing. I went like that for three or four days, sleeping in what TV caves I could find, traveling as long as I could take it each day.

Finally I came to a wisp of cloud. I was right, the clouds were low. They were also made of cotton and they bunched tightly around the top of the pyramid. I pulled the cotton away to make the going easier, and kept climbing.

As I went up, I saw there were hundreds of thin, white strings holding the dark clouds up on either side of me.

I didn't go much farther before I came to a spot where the blue lightning jumped and crackled constantly and swarmed around my head like a halo. The electricity made my hair stand on end and push my hat up so that it seemed to be supported by porcupine quills. The hair on my body poked through my clothes like tacks.

Above me I could see an opening in the blue sky. I went up through that and felt my hair go soft and my hat settle down on my head. When I got through the hole I was at the top of the pyramid and I stepped off of it and found myself inside a tremendous room full of gigantic cameras, sound systems, and gadgets I couldn't identify. None of it looked designed for human hands.

Leaning against a distant wall was a backdrop. It was of the Orbit, and it was the Orbit when it was acidic and the Popcorn King had ruled. My favorite time.

I took the long walk over and touched it. It rippled under my hand and I was able to move into it. It was suddenly real. On the screen nearest me, *Night of the Living Dead* was playing. It wasn't one of the good parts. No one was getting ripped apart or eaten.

There were people moving about among the speakers and cars. They looked stunned, mechanical, thin and wasted. But they didn't look as bad as they were going to look.

When I turned, I expected to be trapped in the Orbit,

and I wouldn't have minded too terribly, but behind me
was a backdrop of the room full of equipment. I reached out
and touched it and walked forward, and I was out of the
Orbit; it was a backdrop again. I was a free agent.

I looked around.

There was this hallway, and on either side of the
hallway were painted backdrops. I went down the hallway
and stopped to look at some of them. One that caught my
eye was of a jungle.

I stepped into it. Immediately I was very hot and the
air was full of the stink of mold and plants, and the trees
were dripping water. I thought maybe this was a backdrop
of the jungle below; maybe by stepping into this one, I was
down below again.

I heard a cracking of trees and brush, and a red, blue
and yellow Triceratops poked its head through some greenery and looked at me. I know they're supposed to be
vegetarians, but I wasn't in the mood to find out. Besides,
he looked as if he might charge. I wondered if he could
charge right out of the backdrop. I turned quickly and
stepped back into the hallway. When I looked at the
backdrop, it was just a jungle. No Triceratops.

I walked down the hallway until a Western backdrop
caught my eye. I stepped into a dusty street and began
walking between rows of clapboard buildings. At the far
end of the narrow street, a tall fellow with a gun on his hip
began walking toward me.

I was dressed for the part, but I didn't like the looks of
this. I turned around and walked back up the street and
stepped back into the hallway.

When I examined the backdrop, there was just an
empty street, of course.

The backdrops came to an end, and in their place were
mirrors that distorted my appearance. No two had me

looking the same. It seemed to me there was some great cosmic truth in this, but try as I might, I couldn't put my finger on it. I kept walking.

The hallway became filled with a large red ball. It towered high above me and touched the walls of the hallway. I put my hand against it and it felt as if it were made of cardboard. I pushed and it rolled back to reveal a split that widened and showed me several rows of jagged, poorly painted, cardboard teeth.

It was the comet that had smiled and turned the Orbit into a horror movie. I pushed the ball hard and it went rolling down the long hallway very fast and disappeared into the distance like the sun falling down the dark shaft of the universe.

I noticed now that the floor beneath me had changed and that I was standing on a dark rectangle and it was in turn linked to another and a series of these went on down the hall and disappeared into the same distance the comet had fallen. On either side and between the rectangles were gaps and out of the gaps poured a bright yellow light that hit against the ceiling.

The light became stronger and warmer. It worked through the rectangle and it worked through me. I fell face forward, went stiff and was enveloped by the flooring.

The light went out.

Lines I remember from my father and his Bible:

In the beginning God created the heaven and the earth. And the earth was without form, and void; and darkness was upon the face of the deep. And the Spirit of God moved upon the face of the waters.

And God said, Let there be light; and there was light.

I don't know about the waters, but there was certainly light, and plenty of it. It was stronger than before and warmer than before; it went through me like new blood. I felt as if I had never lived, except I had memories, and these seemed to belong to someone else and loaned to me. I felt as if I were a new creature in the eyes of the God (or Gods) of film; I was nothing more than a flat lifeless piece of celluloid with a great yellow light shining through me and the light was giving me life.

In other words, I was on a filmstrip.

I could hear gears grinding, sprockets turning, and the rectangle that was my home began to move. It rolled through what must have been a projector, because at some point the bright light became brighter and I hit a white wall and—

I was animated, cartoon style. I held my hand in front of me, and it was black-gloved like it was supposed to be but the hand was puffy and silly, as if it were really nothing more than a glove filled with air.

I was in a little room sitting on a stool, and all around me were white walls, and there were whisperings from somewhere, and occasional shadows, then in front of me was this little blue glow. The glow died down and in its place was a short, dumpy cartoon woman wearing a blue-and-white dress tied in back with a white cloth belt. Her hair was silver and done up in a bun. She was holding a wand tipped with a silver star and she was using it to scratch her ass.

In a voice that had been worked over with Brillo pads, she said, "I think it's the riding around on the film or the light that gives you the itch, but whatever, it's some kind of itch. Lot of us have it. But listen, kid, I'm not here to talk to you about ass itch. We know what you want and we want you to have it. You're made for the part, and I ain't blowing smoke up your ass. You're perfect. You see, the Producer and the Great Director want a show down there and we think you're the one can give it to us. Kid, we're gonna make you a goddamn star."

She took a pack of cigarettes out from under a roll in the sleeve of her dress, shook one out and lipped it, replaced the pack. "We give a man a job, we like to give him the full run of things, see, and while we're talking here, let me tell you something. You're ugly, kid. With a kisser like that if you was a chicken you'd have to sneak up on a pile of shit to peck a corn kernel out of it. But that's not your fault. It's something we can fix."

She brought out a box of wooden matches and struck one on her hip and lit her smoke. She puffed and tossed the box on the floor. She pinched the cigarette between thumb and forefinger and held the flame toward her palm.

"Tell me what face you want, kid. I want to show you what we can do. Naw, don't tell me a thing. I know the face, and it ain't pretty and it ain't ugly. It ain't really a face. You want something everyone will look at. You want it so when you step into a room all eyes go to you. Well, in the name of the Producer and the Great Director, by the power vested in me, and all that stuff, I give it to you."

She waved the wand. "The stuff dreams are made of, kid."

I felt a rush of energy. I was a thermometer and I was overheated and my mercury was about to explode out the top of my head.

Next thing I knew, I was on the floor, then I was coming out of darkness. I blinked and found myself next to the hole that let in the tip of the TV pyramid.

I looked at my hands. They weren't animated now. A big-handled mirror lay next to me. I picked it up and looked at myself.

What I had for a face was a TV, and that suited me fine.

And my face operated like one. Inside my head was the mental switch, and with a twist of my mind I could tune into any movie, television show, commercial, or personal video I wanted.

And I could play it on my face and see it at the same time.

I was proud.

I tossed away the mirror and started down. I felt like Charlton Heston playing Moses in *The Ten Commandments*. But I wasn't coming down from on high with the Ten Commandments. I had something better. Every movie, show and commercial ever made was tucked tight in my head, ready to explode onto my face at a whim.

It took me some time to get down, of course, but when I did, the drive-in was full of people. They had been wandering in for a time. They had built a stage of TVs in front of one of the drive-in screens, and they were taking turns going up there and acting out scenes from movies, quoting dialogue they remembered. They also did sound effects and screams. They weren't too good at it.

When they saw me they stood open-mouthed, and when I turned my face on and filled it with *Night of the Living Dead*, their expressions turned to rapture. I sat down on a TV set and crossed my legs and leaned forward and they gathered before me and squatted down and watched. And when *Night* was over, I gave them *The Texas Chainsaw Massacre* and then *The Sound of Music* intercut with *Zombie*. Now and then I gave them a commercial for GI Joe action figures and accessories, tossed in a California Raisins commercial, and one for some kind of shampoo. Things got cozy.

They loved me, and it was then that I gave myself a new name. I was in Hopalong gear and I had a TV face and my idol had been the Popcorn King, so naturally, I came up with Popalong Cassidy. I told my audience that was what they should call me, and they did. They would have called me anything to keep those images coming; they had learned that the images were the reality and all else was an illusion they had to work to invent. My face did all the work for them. It gave them all the reality they needed to know, minus the effort.

I found that I no longer needed to eat food. All I needed were the eyes and minds of those people on my face. That kept me full.

In time, more people came to the drive-in, and they too sat before my face and worshiped it, and I pulled energy from them and felt fuller and stronger than ever before.

I was loved. Loved by those who sat before me and ate the popcorn and candy that fell from the sky, drank the drinks it rained. Loved, goddamnit, loved. Me, Popalong Cassidy. Loved and admired and revered.

Course, there were some nonbelievers. They wanted to stay away from my face. They saw it as bad. They blamed the movies for what had happened to them.

This was nonsense.

I had my followers rip them open and eat their guts and act out *Night of the Living Dead*. Then the heads of those stupid dissenters went up on tall pieces of antenna and we placed them all around the drive-in as a warning to the nonviewers who might come, and as an inspiration to the rest of us.

I had my followers strike sparks and set the TV pyramid's on fire. They would have no other gods before me. I was it, and I didn't want competition. No one else would be climbing up there to see my Fairy Godmother; no one else could have my prize.

This kept the drive-in a happy place. A new era had dawned. I was its messiah. Offspring of the Producer and the Great Director, whoever they were, and it was my job to make sure they were entertained. And I planned to give my heavenly parents a really big show.

Now let's pause for this brief commercial message.

8

GRACE TALKING

All the while Popalong had been talking, images were flashing on his face. Clips from movies and television shows. Now a series of commercials went lickety-split across the screen; everything from exercise machines to Boxcar Willie's Greatest Hits. Damn if I hadn't always wanted to try Boxcar Willie's stuff, though I hated to admit it. If I ever got home, I was going to order his album.

I suppose there were subliminals at work under all that film stuff, but maybe not. I like to think it had no effect on me because I'm just too much woman to be taken in by a subliminal message; I like to think Mom and Dad raised a pretty stubborn girl and that my martial arts training allowed me to maintain my focus on who I was and what I thought.

Course, maybe the only subliminal in the whole mess was for me to buy a Boxcar Willie album, and that seemed to be working. Maybe all those people who had fallen for Popalong's line of corn were just stupid. My dad always said, "Grace, most people are idiots."

It was kind of cold-blooded, but life seemed to sort of be bearing him out.

The commercials wrapped up, and in spite of myself I liked the last one. It had to do with these carrots, potatoes and bell peppers with stick legs and shoes and stick arms and gloves. They were hopping off the face of a box and dancing across a kitchen table on their way to leap into a pan full of water resting in the mouth of an open stove.

"My message is simple," said Popalong. "There is pleasure in darkness and pain. The light cannot be appreciated without the dark. Entertainment is where it's at. At the end of the highway I have formed a humble Church of Darkness and Pain. Services every day. It all plays on my face. And when someone, shall we say, becomes a star at the church, like those nonbelievers I told you about, we record their acting and play it again and again for our pleasure. No special effects. No wooden lines. No one pretending to eat guts. The real thing. It's addicting, I kid you not."

He leaned close to me. "Revolutionary, don't you think?"

"It bites the moose," I said.

"Now that's ugly," Popalong said. "After all I've shown you and told you, you're still an asshole. I'm afraid you'll have to be edited out of what you call life. But don't worry, I'll make you a star. I'll make sure your agony is recorded forever in the only way that really matters. On film."

He turned to Sue Ellen. "Her, I think she's got potential. I think she can see the light of my face and know it for what it is, don't you? I think she's rather pretty. She might make me a nice queen. I'd like that. I mean I may be a messiah, but to hell with this Jesus stuff where you don't get any pussy. I'm a new kind of messiah, and I say hey, what's the point in being a messiah with all kinds of control, if you don't throw some pork to the women. You see, I can give them any face they want while I make love to them.

Whatever star they want, man or woman, hell, Lassie or Rin Tin Tin, I can call them up on my screen, and presto, I'm who they want me to be."

The rain had stopped and daylight was creeping beneath the tarp and poking through the holes where the rain had come through. The fires in the television sets were dying down and the smoke from them was thinning and becoming lighter, going as soft and gray as the cottony strands of an old man's hair.

The shadows huddling against the back of the tarp were fading. Popalong's shadow was seeping into the ground at his feet like motor oil.

"They're fraidy-cats of the light," he said. "Roy, would you please get the gasoline."

The man who had cut me free climbed on the wrecker and came down with a five-gallon can.

"You should feel honored," Popalong said. "Rare as gasoline is. You know, this will be our last trip out from the church in the wrecker. When we get back we'll be near empty. It's a pisser not to be able to go out and spread the word, but what's a fella to do?"

"You're no fella," I said.

"You know, you're right. Soak her, Roy."

"Don't we get to fuck her first?" Roy asked.

"Now that you mention it," Popalong said, "I do seem to be ahead of myself. Everyone for fucking her?"

He held up his hand as an example. The four men put their hands up.

Popalong turned that sixteen-inch screen on me. "You're popular, what can I say. But you know, I'm going to pass. You have such a nasty disposition, I'm afraid I'd end up having to fake an orgasm. Roy, would you like to be first to crack open the box?"

Roy smiled and put the can down. He got a pair of wire

cutters out of his back pocket and went over and snipped what held me to the wrecker, but this didn't free my hands. They were fastened together by a separate bond.

"You going to record this?" Roy said.

"Whatever I see is recorded," Popalong said. "Bring her out from the wrecker, please, get her pants off, and get started. I'm sort of in a hurry to see her burn. Rest of you get that tarp down."

The three in the back went straight to the tarp and pulled it up and flipped it over the antenna in the middle and tossed it onto the wrecker.

Roy led me so that I was in front of Popalong's antenna. Popalong stepped up on his spokes and hung his arms in the rods. He looked at me and smiled his dials.

"Showtime," he said.

9

There was no wind and the dead air had turned warm and humid. Sweat poured off of me and my hair stuck to the back of my neck. I needed to go to the ladies' room.

Roy wasn't taking me real serious. After all, I was a girl. Maybe I was supposed to beg and scream like in the horror movies.

What I did when Roy reached out to take hold of my pants was swivel on the ball of my left foot and whip my head around and get my hips shifting, and I brought my leg up fast and loose and snapped it back so that the heel caught Roy directly behind his right ear and made a sound like big hands clapping.

Before Roy filled his teeth with dirt, I was moving. One of the men tried to stop me, but I jumped up and snapped out my right leg and caught him in the throat with the edge of my foot. I could feel something in his neck give, then I was down and running, hitting the jungle hard as I could go, keeping my balance best I could, which wasn't easy with my hands tied the way they were. Then I was out of there, boys, prehistoric history.

10

At first I felt like Brer Rabbit in the brier patch, then I didn't feel so good. This was where the film crawled and sucked on you, where the bad storms blew shadows and trees moved.

But nothing of the sort was happening then. The film lay still at my feet and still in the trees. There were no shadows and no storms. I supposed those things were reserved for night.

I heard footsteps behind me and I only paused long enough to jump up and pull my knees to my chest and whip my bound hands underneath me.

I saw that my hands were tied with a piece of wire that had been wrapped around them three or four times with the ends twisted together. I pulled at the wire with my teeth as I ran and got it loose. I crunched it up and put it in my pocket so I wouldn't leave something on the ground for them to mark my passing.

Eventually I didn't hear them anymore, but I kept running. I don't know how long I went, and I had no idea which way I was going. I followed the path of least resistance.

When I felt certain they were no longer behind me, I

stopped and found a tree with low branches and swung up in that and climbed as high as I could.

I was shocked. I had looped back until I was almost to the highway. In fact, I probably wasn't far from where I had been captured. If I had kept running, I would have been out on the highway again in a matter of minutes.

I could see the wrecker at the edge of the highway and I could see Popalong's antenna, but he wasn't on it. I could see the Galaxy too. I couldn't see Popalong, his men or Timothy or Sue Ellen. I could see some dark smoke, but I couldn't tell what it was coming from. Its source was near the edge of the woods though.

I felt poorly, so I found a forked limb that had a lot of leafy cover and wedged my butt in the fork and put my back against a bigger limb and clutched a smaller one with the crook of my right arm. A wind began to stir, and that was all I needed to send me off to dreamland.

When I awoke my back hurt and my arm was stiff, but I felt rested. I had no idea how long I slept. It was still daylight.

I got out on the limb where I had been before and looked at the wrecker. Popalong's antenna cross was in the back of the wrecker, fastened to the wench post somehow, and Popalong was on it. He had this TV head turned in my direction, lifted slightly up, but I didn't think he could see me. One of his men was coiled at his feet like a house cat.

The wrecker started to move. I watched until it was out of sight.

11

At this point, some of this is bound to be obvious. Yes, it was Timothy that was burning. I found the guy I had kicked in the head dead in the bushes. The one I had kicked in the throat had been impaled on a piece of television antenna. Popalong didn't like failures much.

I guess I should have killed Timothy. That's what he asked for. But I got the keys out of my pocket and opened up the trunk of the Galaxy and took the gas can and poured it into the tank. I got my arms under Timothy and got him loaded in the backseat of the Galaxy. His flesh came off on my hands and I had to go out to the side of the road and wipe my palms in the grass; it was as if I had been holding greasy pork chops.

I got the car going and made a U-turn and drove us away from there. I talked about anything that came to mind, and Timothy when he did speak, said, "Kill me."

I didn't seem to know how to do anything but drive, and I did that through the day and through the night, finally stopping to rest. I kept going like that, kept talking and singing and reciting poetry to myself, and I don't remember eating or drinking at all.

There's not much to tell after that. My throat got

hoarse. The road pulled me on. When I was nearly out of gas I saw the lake—your lake—and I guess it made me realize how thirsty I was, and I went for it.

Next thing I knew Jack here was pulling me out and then I was in the back of your camper. I woke up and had to pee, and when I came back from that, you guys were here.

FOURTH REEL

(Titties Even Closer Up, Pants for Jack
and Bob,
and On Down the Road)

1

Bob said, "You're welcome to stay with us."

"Thanks. I appreciate it. But tomorrow, or day after tomorrow, when I'm rested, I'm going to start after Sue Ellen. I owe her that. I went sort of nuts when I found Timothy, panicked, took off in the opposite direction. But I've got to go back now and find her."

"You don't have a car," I said.

"If I can get to Shit Town, I think I can get a car and some gas. If not, I'll go on foot."

"I'm going too," I said.

"What?" Bob said.

"I can't sit here the rest of my life."

"See a set of titties and you go all to pieces, don't you?" Bob said.

"If what she says is true, we know what's at the end of the highway," Crier said. "So why go?"

"Let Grace be the White Knight," Bob said. "She's into that kind of shit. Kung fu lady and all that. We're into surviving."

"I may have to do some ugly things when I catch up to Popalong," Grace said. "It won't be an easy trek, especially if I end up on foot."

123

"Listen to her," Bob said.

"This isn't living," I said. "This is existing. It's giving up. I did that once before. I won't do it again. You're the one made me do something last time, Bob. You're the one pulled me out of just getting by."

"But this isn't so bad," Bob said.

"Maybe we can find a way home at the end of the highway," I said. "Maybe there's something more than what Popalong told her about. And there's that little girl, Sue Ellen."

"I'm not asking anything of any of you," Grace said.

"Not much you're not, lady," Bob said. "You know how to work things. I can see that."

"It's not her fault," I said. "It's what I want."

"Shit," Crier said. "We've been through some things together, the three of us. I feel like we're the three musketeers or something."

"Oh hell," Bob said. "Here it comes."

"We're all we got," Crier said. "I'd like to see us stick together. Hell, fellas, you're the first real friends I ever had."

"Well, fuck," Bob said. "Guess we could use a change of scenery. We can take the camper to Shit Town and try and get some gas there."

"Hey," Grace said. "I'm not asking—"

"Hush," Bob said. "I might come to my senses."

2

Up in Jungle Home I tried to sleep, but no dice. I got out of bed and slipped on my blanket and left Bob and Crier sleeping and went out on the deck where a warm breeze was blowing.

I went on down and walked over to the camper and touched it. It was cool to my touch and I got a mild sexual charge out of it, which made me feel pretty damn silly. I thought about what Grace had said about fucking the ocean in case there was a shark in there that had swallowed a girl, and suddenly it made a lot of sense.

I went around to the end of the camper. The tailgate was down. My mouth filled with saliva. I knew then that I was going to at least look inside.

I looked.

She wasn't there. There was just a basket of fruit. I guess my sexual charge had come from that or a horny spare tire.

Then I heard splashing. I think I had heard it before, but now it registered.

I walked around on the other side of the camper and looked out at the lake.

The moon was high and bright and it made the lake

slick as a mirror. Not too far out in it, halfway submerged, was Grace. She was slapping her arms on the surface of the water. Playing.

I went down there, and when I was fifty feet from the water, I stopped and looked at her sleek, marble-white back sticking out of the water like a flooded Grecian statue.

She looked over her shoulder and smiled.

"Out for a walk, Jack?"

"Sort of."

"Excited about tomorrow?"

"I guess."

"You saved my life today."

"That's all right."

"Of course it is. I got hot in the camper. Funny, Timothy's down at the other end of the lake and here I am playing in the water at this end. I never made love to him, you know."

"Did you want to?"

"I think I saw him as a brother."

"You telling me this for a reason?"

"I don't know."

She turned and started to shore. She came out of the water like Venus being born. The moon hit the sheen of water on her breasts and made them bright as moons themselves. The little pink stripes on her skin looked like birthday ribbons.

"You're going to go blind," she said.

"I don't make you go naked."

"I didn't make you come down here."

I put my hands in front of me and clasped them together.

She came to me and kissed me lightly on the lips. Her breath smelled of fruit. She took hold of my arms, lifted them over her head and around her neck, said, "You'll have to pull out, you know. I don't have any birth control. And don't make more of this than it is."

I pulled her to me and kissed her. Our tongues made war.

She looked down. "Goodness, Jack. There's something in your blanket."

"You've already seen it. You weren't much impressed."

She took hold of the edges of the blanket and pulled it over my head, knocking my arms off of her. She threw the blanket down on the grass and took hold of me.

"My," she said, "how the little fella's grown."

3

After we made love on my blanket, we stumbled giggling to the camper and smeared fruit on one another and licked it off. Between licking and giggling, we made love again. Every time we moved apart our bodies made a sound like two sheets of flypaper being pulled apart.

When we finished we went down to the lake and rinsed off again and tried to make love again, but neither of us was up to it. We went back to the camper and fell asleep in each other's arms.

I dreamed good for a time. Kind of dreams a man dreams when he's holding a woman in his arms. But the dreams didn't last. I thought about my aliens and I thought about Grace's story about Popalong Cassidy and the Producer and the Great Director. I thought about all that movie junk on down the highway. I tried to make everything add up but nothing would.

It all went away and folded into a cloud the color and texture of Grace's pubic hair.

Next morning Bob woke me by pulling on my foot. I got my head out from between Grace's legs and looked up.

"That's disgusting, you know," Bob said.

I picked up Grace's shirt from the floorboard and draped it over her. I got my clothes and sat out on the tailgate and put them on.

"Well, I hope we enjoyed ourselves," Bob said.

"We did."

Bob went away and I woke Grace up and she got dressed and we helped Crier and Bob load some fruit and bamboo water containers in the camper. Then we were off.

After a few days we came to Shit Town. The post Grace had told us about was gone, and now there was an official sign made of crude lumber. On it was: SHIT TOWN, POPULATION: WHO GIVES A FUCK.

Civic pride.

Shit Town wasn't much. Some shacks made of sticks and crooked lumber mostly. It looked like a place the Big Bad Wolf would blow down.

Out next to the road was a line of cars, and people were living in those too. Some of the cars were fixed up with huts connected to them. Snazzy stuff.

We parked on the opposite side of the highway, locked up and walked over to Main Street, which was a dirt track, and went down it.

A few people ogled us, and we ogled them back.

No one offered us the Key to the City.

In spite of Shit Town not looking like much, I suppose by present standards it's pretty prosperous. There were a lot of people moving about and there was an aura of industry in the air.

Down at the end of the street was a well house. Most likely it had been built over an open spring, as I figured that was what had attracted folks to this spot in the first place, as the lake had attracted us to Jungle Home.

Beyond this I could see a lot of stumps leading to the

jungle. In a short time, with only their hands and crude tools, these people had cut a lot of trees.

I figured eventually this kind of industry would lead to Shit Town having burger joints that served dinosaur and rabbit burgers, and eventually the place might move up the evolutionary line to having a kind of thrift store where you could get shower curtains, house shoes, bird feeders and Bermuda shorts.

A lot of women were pregnant, and though I'm not good at guessing things like that, they looked pretty close to domino date to me. Of course, time here is too hard to judge.

There were little huts along the street and some of them had plank counters out front with things to trade on them. There was one that had flat-in-the-middle green bread with flies on it, and behind the counter was this woman leaning on a hut post with her dress hiked up and her butt free to the air. There was a guy with his pants down against her, and he was putting it to her. If the woman liked it, it didn't show, and the fella looked like a man called to duty.

It didn't take long, and when they finished, she let down her dress and took the loaf of bread and went away. The man pulled up his pants and looked at us.

"Ya'll want bread?"

"I don't think so," Bob said.

We went on down the street and came to another stand, and on its counter was a turtle shell turned upside down, and there was a wooden pestle in it. All around the shell were piles of fruit.

A guy with a belly that looked like a bag of rocks under his shirt got off a stump when he saw us coming and came over and smiled at us. All this teeth had gone south except

one dead center of his bottom gum. The rest of him didn't
look too good either.

"Want me to make you a fruit drink?" he said. "Mashed
right here while you wait."

"Nope," Crier said.

Next to the fruit juice place was a hut with a sign out
front painted in black mud that read: LIBRARY.

"They're kidding," Bob said.

I went over and pulled the curtain of reeds aside and
looked in. There was just enough room for one person in
there, and that one person had to sit on a rotting stump
because the roof was low. There was one crude shelf of
books, and under the shelf was a little sign that said: PLEASE
RETURN BOOKS.

I went inside and looked at what they had to offer.
There was a Bible covered in red plastic with a zipper on it.
I unzipped it and looked inside. Saw that everything Jesus
had said was printed in red so you could tell it from ol'
So-and-So.

Alongside it was a collection of Rod McKuen's poetry,
and a copy of *Jonathan Livingston Seagull* with "This book
belongs to David Webb and is his inspiration" written
inside.

There were two copies of the *Watchtower*, one con-
centrating on the dilemmas of dating in the modern world,
the other on the deterioration of the family unit.

There was also a pamphlet for raising chinchillas for
fun and profit (neither the fun or profit being to the
advantage of the chinchillas); a postcard with a gerbil's
picture on the front and a note on the back that said they
could be seen at some petting zoo; a photo-novel of
Superman 3; and a souvenir hand fan from Graceland with
a picture of the erstwhile King of Rock'n'Roll on one side
(prebloat) and the words to "You Ain't Nothing But A

Hound Dog" on the other. There were also a couple of
poems that didn't rhyme written on some dirty popcorn
bags with eyeliner pencil.

I took the Elvis fan and fanned myself, then put it back
and went outside. The others had wandered down the
street, not having felt the pull of the arts.

The guy with the one tooth said, "Find anything?"

"I fanned myself a little."

"It's checked out right now, but there's a pretty good
Max Brand novel we got, 'cept the last couple of pages are
torn out. Some fella wrote an ending for it, though. He
wrote on the inside back cover, 'He rode off into the West
and everything was okay.' Seems a good enough ending to
most anything, don't it?"

"Does at that. I take it you're also the librarian?"

"Yeah, but people want fruit juice more than they want
books. Only thing is they don't always have something good
to trade. Tell you, I've had all the dry pussy I want. It's
making the head of my dick raw. In the long run I get the
bad end of the trade. I'd really rather have some kind of
meat, fish, maybe some roots that are good to boil."

"Commerce can be a bitch," I said.

4

When I caught up with the others, they were standing beside the street looking out between a couple of shacks made of mud and sticks, staring at a man hanging from the limb of a big oak tree. He was spinning around, kicking his feet and working his elbows as if in a square dance. The elbows were all he could work of his arms, since his hands were tied behind his back.

On a bench near the oak sat two men and a woman. They looked like benched football players waiting for their turn at an inning.

"Suicide tree I told you about," Grace said. "Come on."

"I don't want to see that," I said.

"Me neither," Bob said.

"I'll pass too," Crier said.

"Do what you want," Grace said to me, "but they're going to hang themselves anyway and you fellas need pants."

"Pants?" I said.

"You think those folks are gonna need them later?"

"I got pants," Crier said. "They're ragged, but they're pants. I'll just hang out."

Grace led Bob and me over to the tree. I looked up at the guy. His face was purple as a plum and his neck was swollen out in such a way it was starting to spread over the rope. His tongue was flopping against his chin and he was biting through it. His eyes were crossed and the lid of one was drooped halfway down and the other eye looked like a table tennis ball being pushed out of a hole from behind.

We went over to the bench. The woman was sitting on the end near us and the men were sitting next to each other. She looked at us. The hair on one side of her head had been burned off, and the hair on the other side wasn't anything to be proud of. It was dirty-brown and kinky as wire. I've seen Brillo pads with more class. She had on a filthy T-shirt and her nipples were punching through it. The jeans she had on were thin enough to shit through. Her face wasn't any kind of special. It was covered with pimples and red welts. She was barefoot.

The two guys weren't fashion models either. They had beards full of dirt, bugs and fruit seeds. Their dark coloring wasn't the result of the sun's rays. You could have packed lunches in the pores of their skin.

I hated to think what I looked like.

"Bench is full," the woman said. "Come back tomorrow. Three's about it for a day. Them's the rules."

"We're not here to hang ourselves," Grace said.

"If you're going to watch," she said, "stay back out of the way. This bastard won't never choke. I bet he's been up there an hour."

"He looks about gone to me," I said.

The man beside her, the skinnier of the two, said, "Who can tell how long he's been up there. Time isn't worth a duck fart here. But you should have seen him just a little while ago. He looked worse than this. I think he's gotten him a second wind."

"Maybe he's changed his mind," I said.

At that the hanging man began to kick his legs vigorously.

"I don't think so," the woman said.

"Look at him," I said.

"You can't pay that any mind. It doesn't mean a thing. He wanted to go worse than the rest of us. He bit Clarence there to get first in line."

Clarence was the skinny fella. He held up a sticklike arm and pushed his short sleeve back. There was a crescent of teeth wounds.

"He called me some things I've never heard," said Clarence, "then he pushed me on the ground and bit me. I told him to go ahead. Hell, I wasn't even next in line. Fran was. But look who he bit. That's the way it's always been for me. I tied his hands for him and boosted him into the rope. More than he deserved, I'll tell you. Which reminds me, you folks around when Gene here goes, maybe you could tie his hands for him. It works better that way, otherwise you claw at the rope, no matter how bad you want to go."

"I'll make do," Gene said. He got up and went over to the hanging man and jumped on him and swung back and forth like a kid on a tire swing. The hanging man's neck lengthened.

"We probably won't be around long enough to help Gene," Grace said, "but we wanted to try and talk you out of your pants, just you fellas. Jack and Bob here don't have anything but these dresses."

"Noticed that," Clarence said, "and I'll tell you boys, you haven't got the legs for it."

From the hanging man came a sound like a semi tire blowing out at high speed.

"Goddamn," Clarence said, "there's the signal."

"Yeah," Fran said. "It's nature's way of saying '*Sayonara*, motherfucker.'"

"It's nature's way of filling your pants with shit, is what it is," Clarence said. "Get off of him, Gene. Let's get him down and get Fran up there. Come on, get off of him, goddamnit."

"About those pants," Grace said.

"Guess you want them before I hang myself," Clarence said.

"Well," Grace said, "you know how it is, nature's *sayonara* and all."

Clarence nodded and undressed. He didn't have on any underwear. He tossed the clothes at me. "Take all of it. Shoes too, if they fit. Hell, if they don't fit."

I gathered up the clothes and held them. They smelled a little ripe.

"Hey Gene," Clarence said. "Want to help the other fella out?"

Gene had finally got off the dead man, and he came over to the bench and sat down. He took off his clothes, except for some soiled, green boxer shorts, and gave them to Bob.

"Go on, enjoy them," Clarence said. "You want to thank us later, well, we'll be hanging around."

Clarence loved that. He laughed like a drunk hyena.

He was tying Fran's hands for her when we went away.

5

We collected Crier and went out to the camper. He and Grace sat up front and talked, and Bob and I tried the clothes on. I ended up with some pants too tight in the waist, but I zipped them up high as they would go and left them unsnapped and used the belt I had made for my blanket outfit and ran it through the pants loops for extra support. The shirt fit fine and I wore it with the tails hanging out. The socks were thin but not holey. The shoes were an inch too long and they made me look a little like Bozo the Clown.

Bob's pants fit him in the waist, but were too short. They were what my dad used to call high-water pants. The shirt he had was too narrow across the shoulders, and he got a knife out of the toolbox and slit it halfway down the back. He slit the sides of the shoes too because they were too narrow.

Grace and Crier laughed at our outfits, but just a little. I guess thinking about where the clothes came from took some of the humor out of it.

Crier and Bob stayed with the camper, and Grace and I took Bob's gas can and went around begging for gas. The people who were living in cars that had huts attached to them were the quickest to give up their gas; they had made a stand and they were staying. Some wouldn't even talk to us, and one guy told us he'd pour his goddamn gas on the ground and piss on it before he gave it to us. We took this as a no.

By the end of the day we had a full tank of gas, and we went into Shit Town one last time to see if we could talk someone into giving us enough to fill our can. It never hurt to have extra.

We got off Main Street and went down a little side street lined with huts and cars and we came on this tall, hatchet-faced fella wearing a sweat-stained cowboy hat. He was unusual in that he was clean-shaven.

He had the hood up on an old red-and-white Plymouth convertible, and he had a wrench and he was fiddling with something under there. He didn't look like someone that wanted to get rid of his gas, but we asked anyway.

"I got plans for a big trip," he said. "Need all the gas I can get. Y'all want a drink? It's the local poison. Made out of fruit juice and piss. No kidding. It'll put you higher than goddamn Skylab."

We passed.

He took a swig and shivered. "Things a man'll drink. Look here, name's Steve."

He stuck out his hand and we took turns shaking it and giving our names.

"Guess y'all are heading on down the highway too, huh?"

"That's the plan," I said.

"Maybe I'll see you then. Soon as I get this buddy tuned up, have me a damn good drunk, I'll be ready to roll. I figure sometime tomorrow. Can't say that I see much to keep me here."

We wished him luck and went back to the camper without the gas. I didn't look in the direction of the hanging tree.

It was dark by the time we got back there, and the four of us talked and ate some fruit and went to bed. Crier slept in the front seat as usual, and Bob, Grace and I slept in the back.

Grace was between me and Bob, but she didn't try to molest me, and she didn't try and molest Bob. Bob refrained from playing with himself.

I lay there and thought about Grace and told myself I was too mature and philosophical and had been through too much to expect anything of our relationship other than friendship. Besides, hadn't she said not to make too much of the other night?

Some things you just had to take like an adult. What she did was what she did and it didn't matter to me. She was her own person. And a man's got to do what a man's got to do, and look and see if you're right then go ahead, and every dog has his day, and every cloud has a silver lining, and a penny saved is a penny earned, and everything works out for the best, and . . . it was a long night.

It was later than we planned by the time we got up. We had fruit for breakfast because there wasn't any ham and eggs and coffee on the menu, then we got out of there. Crier and Bob up front, me and Grace in the back.

Grace talked about some books I hadn't read and necking didn't come up.

That's how it went for a few days, and finally I quit worrying about IT every second, and cut down to about once an hour.

So when I wasn't thinking about IT, I was thinking

about what in hell had possessed me to agree to go along on
this little run. I wasn't any hero. I had tried to be once and
I had gotten nailed up for the trouble. What I did best was
mind my own business, and here I was barreling down the
highway so I could confront Popalong Cassidy, who did not
sound like a nice guy. Worse yet, I was the reason Crier and
Bob were going too. Or at least part of it. I guess when a
fella gets bored he can do some stupid things. And maybe
I thought I was being macho going with Grace to the end of
the highway to help her out. I was wondering how I had
ever arrived at that. Grace could probably beat up all three
of us.

Damn, Bob had been right when he said a set of titties
made me go all to pieces. And maybe Grace had known
exactly what she was doing that night in the camper and
down by the lake—sealing a deal.

And maybe I was being a horse's ass. It really hurt to
discover I had a bigger streak of male chauvinist pig in me
than I thought. It hurt worse to realize that I was stupid and
tittie blind and was probably going to get killed for it. I
preferred happy endings.

But even this kind of thinking didn't last. You can only
focus on your own death and destruction so long before it
gets boring. You begin to wonder about more important
matters, like do people who wear suspenders wear them
because they like the way they look, or because they hold
their pants up? Do people who work on garbage trucks see
their work as important? Did they grow up wanting to be
garbage men? What kind of tools are used to scrape dead
animals off the highway? Who was the idiot who invented
those Happy Face symbols, or those signs that read BABY ON
BOARD or SHIT HAPPENS? Should those folks be slow-tortured

by parboiling, or killed outright? What was the true story
on green M&M's?

I tell you, I had lots of interesting things to think
about.

6

That night we got some dried brush and stuff and used our flint and steel to build a little fire near the camper, and pretty soon it was a big fire because Bob couldn't get warm enough and he kept piling brush on it.

"You're gonna catch the truck on fire," Crier said.

"No, I ain't," Bob said. "We're right here in front of the fire."

"I won't burn up to save the truck," Crier said.

"Count me out too," Grace said.

"It's all right," Bob said. "I'm watching it."

After that we sat there and thought and said a little now and then, but not too much because we had our minds on some things, like the fact the highway was starting to change. The nights were getting darker, as if the air was getting thicker, and there were posters and popcorn bags and soft drink cups and the like lying about, and I figured pretty soon we'd be getting into the stormy part. Already we were seeing things in the truck mirrors, and sometimes things reflected in the windows; things like the face of King Kong, the Frankenstein monster clinging to the side of the truck, Dracula and Daffy Duck with their arms around one another.

It was pretty disconcerting to see stuff like that, then look and not find anything there to reflect it. On second thought, I guess we were glad of that. Still, it was unnerving.

Anyway, we were sitting there, and Crier said, "Got to see a man about a horse."

"Me too," I said.

We walked out behind the truck and stood in the highway to do our business. It was very dark. I looked down the road the way we had come. There was a bend in the road and it went around behind some trees and there was some moonlight on the highway, but when I looked in the other direction it was dark as the inside of a goat.

I finished pissing and put my equipment up and wandered off the highway and started walking along the edge in the direction of the dark part. I didn't go too far. It was really dark.

I turned and looked at Crier. He was still hosing the concrete. He looked at me and said, "You know, after all we've been through, bad as it's been, I think things are about to get better. I feel it."

I was going to say something to that, but around the corner came two headlights and the faintest glint of a grillwork smile.

Crier, dong in hand, swiveled in the direction of the car and then he was a hood ornament.

The car, a convertible, sailed by me with Crier bent over the hood and the driver hit down on the horn, stomped the brakes and yelled, "Motherfucker!"

Crier went under the car and bounced out from beneath it and lay in the highway with the moonlight for a shroud. He still had his dong in his hand, but it wasn't connected to his body anymore. He had jerked it off, no pun intended. Lying on his back, his fist on his chest, his dong clenched there like a frankfurter, he looked as if he were studying the universe while preparing to eat a weenie.

FIFTH REEL

(Tooling With Steve, Crier Gets Some Sunglasses,
Showdown at the Orbit)

1

The convertible fishtailed to a stop, disappearing into the darker part of the highway, and right before it did, I caught the ghostly reflection of something in one of its mirrors, some kind of monster that faded with the car's movement. Then the driver was out of the car and running toward Crier. I knew the moment I saw his cowboy hat that it was Steve from back at Shit Town.

I got my feet out of the glue and started over to Crier. Steve was down on his knees feeling Crier's chest and neck. He looked up at me and said, "Dead as a rock."

I tried to kick Steve in the face, but he caught my foot and pulled me on my butt.

"I didn't do it on purpose," he said.

I tried to get up and swarm him. He jabbed me in the chest with his palm and knocked me on my butt again.

"I didn't see him. He shouldn't have been standing in the highway."

"You sonofabitch. You goddamn sonofabitch."

Bob and Grace came over. As they neared us they slowed down, as if taking small steps would give the reality of the thing time to go away.

When they stood over us and looked down, Bob said, "Damn. One thing after another."

"One of you get his feet," Steve said, "and let's get him out of the road before we get creamed by somebody."

Grace got Crier's feet and Steve got him under the arms and they started him off the highway. Crier's hand fell off his chest and he dropped what he was holding.

"Put him down," Steve said.

They lowered him to the highway and Steve picked up what Crier had dropped and put it in Crier's shirt pocket. It poked out the top like a periscope.

They picked him up again and carried him over to the side of the road, and Steve went and got in his car and pulled it over to our side and walked back to us. I kept thinking I'd find something on the ground to pick up and hit Steve with, but the urge was going away. There didn't seem to be any reason to hit anyone.

Grace didn't feel that way. She kicked Steve flush in the balls. He dropped to his knees and had a facial workout. When that was over and he got his breath back, he said, "Damn, lady."

"It didn't make me feel as good as I hoped," Grace said, "but it still does a little something for me."

Then the camper blew up.

2

Hot, sticky morning with the convertible's tape deck blasting Sleepy LaBeef who's singing something about how he's a boogie-woogie man, jetting along with the top down, doing about ninety plus, me in the front seat, Steve at the wheel, bugs on the windshield, Grace, Bob and Crier in the back. Crier strapped in with a seat belt, leaning to the left, head partly out the window, hair standing up like wire, eyelids blown back by the wind, eyes glassy as cheap beads, pecker in his pocket, the tip of it shriveling and turning brown.

"Oh no," Grace says, "the fire's all right. It isn't too big. Nosir. Just right. I'm in front of it. No problem. It's not too close to the truck. Ol' Bob's got it under control. Ol' Bob's got it by the balls. Ol' Bob—"

"Shut up, will you," Bob says.

Steve sings along with Sleepy LaBeef. New bugs hit the windshield. Outside the scenery is changing. More popcorn bags and garish posters lying about, blowing up as we jet by. The trees are starting to fill with film. Broken TV sets and fragments of antennas clutter the side of the road. Crier's pecker continues to wither.

Steve moves the convertible up to a hundred and it's rocking a little. The sun is glinting off the hood and the tires are whining. I hope no one is standing in the road. All seats are taken.

3

High noon and we ran out of Sleepy LaBeef. Then we got Steve.

"Now the reason I'm here is my wife. Finding out your gal can work a dick better than Tom Mix could work a lariat is all right, but the bad news on a thing like that is finding out the dick she works best don't belong to you. Wrong cow pony, you know. It can deflate a man's ego."

"What about you?" Grace said.

"Oh yeah," Steve said, not catching her tone. "Especially when all I ever got was the old in-and-out and are-you-finished-yet."

"Imagine that," Grace said.

"Worse than that, her man was none other than Fred Trual, and that goddamn got me, I'll tell you. He's a real baboon's ass, all the personality of a snot rag and as loyal as a paid-for date. He also stole my song 'My Baby Done Done Me Wrong,' and that was enough for me to swear I'd kill him.

"How in hell do you figure a woman. This Fred is not only ugly, but he's been in the pen and rumor has it he poisoned his old maiden aunt for what she was gonna leave him, and he knew that wasn't nothing but five hundred dollars. I mean we're talking a greedy sonofabitch here. He even eats until he gets sick. I've known him since grade school. Wasn't worth a damn then either. But the gals always went for him. Must have had some kind of smell that got to them. Had to be that. He wasn't pretty and he wasn't smart and he wasn't nice. He and Tina Sue even stole my car."

"See you got it back," I said. "Are you sure we heard both sides of Sleepy?"

"About three times to a side," Steve said. "I got it back all right, but not because they gave it to me. I'll tell you about it."

"That's all right," Grace said. "No need to bother."

"I don't mind," Steve said, and he made a corner and the tires screeched like startled owls. "I told myself when I caught up with them I was going to kill Fred. I thought I might even kill her too. And I thought when they were both dead I was going to get out my guitar and sing the song I wrote over their dead bodies, then maybe on the back of my guitar I'd write another one in their blood, right then and there. That's how mad I was. Nasty, huh."

"You're not a nice fella, Steve," Bob said.

"Now I didn't mean to run over that ol' boy, I swear it. I'm a sensitive fella, don't think I'm not. I mean I can write the kind of songs that make the whiningest, sorriest-living, beer-drinkingest and gal-losingest sonofabitch cry like a baby with a thermometer up its ass. Kind of song that'll make women's thangs tingle and make fellas call home to make sure their old ladies aren't doing it with the next-door neighbor. Know what I mean?"

"I think you sort of summed it up there," Bob said.

"It'll make me a rich man. Or would if we were back in the real world. I'd be able to buy clothes that aren't on sale at the goddamn K mart. Go to some place to buy stuff that ain't made out of genuine plastic and genuine cheap. I'd be able to get me a new hat made out of real hat stuff and have it be one of those with a fancy band around it with a feather fresh out of a peacock's ass sticking up in it. I'd get me some unchewed toothpicks to stick in the band. I'd move to Nashville and sing my sexy little heart out. I'd wine and dine and chase them honky-tonk angels until my dick needed a wheelchair to get around. Course, that's what I would have done. I reckon Fred's made a mint off it now. It's probably on the radio back home. Go in any joint with a juke and I bet you can hear my song coming out of it, probably sung by George Jones or Randy Travis. And ol' Fred's spending my money. Tell you, I still want to kill him. If I got the chance I'd kill him deader than the ol' boy in the back seat there, then I'd really get rough."

"I take it you don't like Fred," Bob said.

"You're getting it. Let me backtrack on my story here."

"I thought that was all of it," Grace said. "I mean that's enough to hold me. What about you guys?"

"I want to hear it all," Bob said.

I was starting to get interested too, but I didn't say anything. I didn't want Grace to kick me in the balls.

"Well, when I found out Fred and Tina Sue were doing what they were doing from this private detective fella I hired, I couldn't hardly believe it. 'Cept that he had some real clear pictures of them in action and he didn't help matters none by saying stuff like, 'That's her best shot there, the one with the whip and the Mousketeer hat,' and 'By God, I didn't know human bodies could do them sort of things. Hell, I didn't know snakes could do them sort of things. Look at that, will you. I bet he's got his head halfway in there, whadaya think?'

"I wasn't just hurt that Tina Sue was waxing another man's rope, or that the man was stupid, greedy, and maybe

a murderer. There was the fact that Fred seemed to be
having a hell of a lot better time with Tina Sue than I'd ever
had. I didn't even know she had a Mousketeer hat. To put
it simple, I was charmed by them sweet little eight-by-ten
color glossies. Here I was busting chops and sweating
gravel just to make a living, trying to write songs on the side
so I could be a country-and-western singer, making the
occasional trip to Nashville to try and peddle my songs—
and not having much luck with it—and I find out my
suspicions about my wife are true, and worse, it's old Fred
and he's having a better time than me. Then to put the
goddamn Howdy Doody smile on it, I found out they not
only went off together in my car, but took my song on
account of Fred claimed he wrote it some years back and I
won it from him in a poker game. I only played poker with
Fred and them other boys a few times, and I didn't never
win. Come to think of it, I think Fred cheats.

"Anyway, I got all this from the note."

The wind was picking up and posters and cups and
popcorn bags were tornadoing around the car and beginning to collect on the windshield and flutter into the seats
and slap Crier in the face.

Steve pulled over and put the convertible's roof up and
Bob took the bags off Crier's face and tossed them out. Back
on the road, Steve continued his story.

"The note was stuck in the refrigerator door when I got
home, on account of the bitch took all the fruit magnets
with her. Even the one I bought for myself that was made
like a big strawberry. The note said what she had done and
that she thought the car was as much hers as mine (which
was a hoot) and that the new song I said I wrote and was
bragging about I didn't write, 'cause her boyfriend did, and
she said she and the boyfriend were heading to Nashville to
make the money off of it. She said she thought it was a

better song than she thought before, now that she knew I
didn't write it. She said good-bye and that she had popped
the tops on all the beer in the refrigerator so it would go
flat, and for me to take a water hose and run it up my ass
and turn it on full blast.

"I tell you, there wasn't a cheerful line in that note. I
of course went straight on over to Fred's. I was back a day
earlier than they expected. I had been up to Nashville, see,
and I come back early to check with the private detective
guy, and to see if I could talk some things out if my
suspicions were correct, so I figured I just might get the
jump on them two before they were gone with my song.

"Thinking that I had left my convertible with Tina Sue
and drove her damned old VW up to Nashville didn't make
me no happier, and I tell you when I got up in Fred's yard
and seen my Plymouth sitting there, the sides of it all
muddy and the hubcaps covered over with the stuff, my
eyes filled with murder. I slammed on my brakes hard
enough to throw my hat in the backseat. I got that dude
back on my head and went straight up on Fred's porch. Last
year's Christmas wreath was still hanging on the door; one
of them with the plastic mistletoe and those damned ol'
gold-sprayed pine cones glued on it. I jerked that little
buddy off the door and stomped the cones and kicked the
rest of it out in the yard.

"One of Fred's old two-bit hounds come around from
the back then and stood off the porch growling at me. I got
hold of Fred's sandy old doormat and threw it at the dog
and it ran off under the house where it could collect some
more ticks.

"About the time I turned around, I saw that the curtain
over one of the windows was falling back into place, and I
knew then that Fred was home. The window he'd taken a
peek out of had MERRY CHRISTMAS stenciled on it, and I yelled

out, 'I know goddamn good and well you're in there, shit-bag. Come on out. And it ain't even Christmas, you dumb cocksucker.'

"He didn't come out, so I got off the porch and got hold of the cinder block he was using for a step and put it on the porch, got up there and got hold of it again and shoved it through the window with the stenciling on it.

"He come out of there then with a chair leg in his hand, and he come out swinging. We sort of run together and rolled off the porch and out in the yard. His old hound come out from under the porch then and got hold of my pants leg and started growling and tugging on it. I kicked the mutt off and wrestled up to my feet, and thought I was going to do pretty good, when Fred hit me one on the noggin with that chair leg, and the last thing I remembered was the toes of my K mart boots coming up."

"But it didn't kill you," Grace said.

"No it didn't. I woke up and the first thing I seen when I got up on my elbow was the toes of them boots again."

"And they were still from K mart," Grace said.

"Still from K mart. But the knot on my head was from Fred. Next thing I see is Fred and that hound dog. The dog is sitting on his butt staring at me, his ol' tongue hanging out like he just had him a bitch and was damn proud of it, and Fred he still has his chair leg, and he bends over me and says, 'Hurt much, Steve?'

"I tell him, 'Not at all. Sometimes when I'm home I take a chair leg to my own head.'

"He hit me again, and when I woke up, I was hot and it was dark and crowded and I could smell that perfume Tina Sue always wore."

Steve paused and pointed at the glove box. "I got a last cigar in there. Been saving it. Get it for me, will you?"

I got it out and he bit off the end and spat tobacco out

the window and put the cigar in his mouth and sucked on it. "I don't care what they say, these things taste a hell of a lot better when you know they ain't made by a bunch of Cubans."

He punched in the lighter.

"All right, damnit," Grace said. "What was this dark, cramped place that smelled like Tina Sue?"

"I'm gonna tell you." He took the lighter and lit the cigar, puffed dramatically. "The trunk of this car."

"Uh oh," Bob said.

"Uh oh is right. The greedy sonofabitch had shown his true colors. I figure he decided he wasn't gonna share any song money with Tina Sue, and he killed her. Then I come along and he had to kill me—least he thought he killed me. And he put us in the trunk of the car and drove us out to the Orbit and walked off, probably hitched home. It wasn't such a smart idea, really. I mean someone would have caught up with him. But then whatever happened to the drive-in happened, and I was trapped in there, and I guess back home in Texas there isn't even a drive-in no more. I don't know what would be there in its place, if anything. But there's no body in the trunk for the police to find, in fact there's no car. So I guess Fred did all right by accident. He's probably making money off my song right now."

"Look at it this way," Bob said. "Maybe the song wasn't any good and he couldn't sell it."

Steve sat and thought about that. The fire on his cigar went out. Finally he said, "I'm not sure how I feel about that."

"What I want to know," Grace said, "is how did you get out of the trunk?"

"Oh, that. Wasn't nothing to that. I was hot and pissed and I bent up my legs and kept donkey-kicking the trunk till I busted the lock. When I got out of there didn't nobody care, things being like they were. I ended up using some wire I had back there to fasten the trunk down."

"Is Tina Sue . . . you know?" Grace said.

"Back there? Naw. I left here there a while, but when things got real bad back there, well, I ate her."

4

After a time, even Steve played out. Course, we had gotten most of his life story, and I guess maybe there wasn't much else to tell. The story wasn't exactly exemplary. I couldn't see it as a movie. He sang us a few of the songs he'd written. Nashville wasn't missing anything. Grace said it all sounded like "Home on the Range" to her, no matter what words he sang. He got quiet then, went into one of those artistic funks, no doubt. He made corners faster than ever and he wouldn't play the Sleepy LaBeef tape.

I had a hard time relaxing, way Steve was driving. And I was thinking about Crier and his dead eyeballs getting whipped by the wind. I knew it wasn't a thing to get on Crier's nerves, but it was damn sure giving mine a workout, and I didn't even have to look at him. Still, the thought of those dead eyeballs behind me . . .

When Steve had asked for that cigar, I had seen that there were some sunglasses in the glove box, and I got those out. They were neon yellow and had little bulldogs in the top corners of the frames and the dogs had black BB eyes that rolled around at the slightest movement. It wasn't exactly what I was looking for, but it was something.

I handed them back to Bob and told him what I

wanted, and he put them on Crier. It helped. Crier even looked alive. He appeared to be nothing more than an excessively cool dude with his dick in his pocket.

Course, a little later in the day he started to bloat up and stink a little, and I couldn't think of anything to help that. We had to pull over and put him in the trunk, sunglasses and all. Steve fussed about this, because he had to work at unwiring the lid, but he did it. I think he was afraid if he didn't, Grace would kick him in the balls. She had that look.

We got Crier dumped in the back without his dick falling out of his pocket, got him wired in, and we were off. It seemed strange not to have the old boy with us, after all we had been through, but it did smell a mite fresher, especially to Bob and Grace.

It got darker and darker and pretty soon we got to that stuff Grace told us about. Storms whipped posters and popcorn sacks and the like every which way. The moon looked even more false than usual and it shone like a projector light through the trees, hitting the strips of film that twisted and twined there. Film ghosts were no longer reflected in the mirror and the windows. The highway was full of them: cowboys with six-shooters, knights with swords and lances, apes and madmen, giant stalking machines from *War of the Worlds*, the smiling Brady Bunch. We drove through them all as if they were mist.

Film strips crawled onto the highway and made smashed cellophane sounds beneath our tires.

When Steve got tired, we pulled over and I got behind the wheel. I drove until I couldn't, then I swapped with Bob who drove until he had to swap with Grace.

When it got back around to me, the gas gauge showed a quarter tank.

5

Daylight, and things looked a little better. No ghosts melting through the car, and no film crawling. A little storm activity, but nothing special. The sun looked worse than ever, like a pie pan spray-painted gold.

The trees were rubbery-looking and the ground reminded me of Styrofoam. The fruit we found to eat was shriveled and bitter to the taste. Everything around us looked a little cheap and off center, like the way it is when you make a real close examination of what you bought at a thrift sale.

We found a few chocolate almonds lying about and some soft drink puddles, so I knew we were getting close to the highway's end; the place Popalong had told Grace about. It struck me that Steve ought to know what he was in for. All he knew was that he was giving us a ride to the end of the highway. He didn't know we had some idea what was there, and he didn't know what we had in mind.

Steve had a mirror in his glove box, one of those kinds with the props behind it, and he had that and his pocket knife and a little kit with a tiny pair of scissors and a toenail clipper in it, and he was working on his whiskers. It made me hurt to watch him.

"Who you cleaning up for?" Bob asked him.

"Myself. I never could stand whiskers. I still don't look so good when I finish, since I can't get close enough, but it beats looking like you boys."

"I think we ought to explain something to you," I said.

"About what?" Steve said. He finished up and folded the mirror stand and put it and the kit in the glove box.

"About the end of the road," Grace said.

Steve leaned on the car and got what was left of his cigar out of his pocket. When it died out he hadn't relit it. He didn't light it now. He put it in his mouth and rolled it from one side to the other.

"We kind of know what's at the end," Grace said. "We've got an idea what we're going to do there." And she told Steve a condensed version of the story she told us. When she finished Steve quit moving his cigar. He took it out of his mouth and put it in his pocket. I couldn't help but think of Crier's dick.

"Sounds like you folks are going to get killed, is what it sounds like to me," Steve said.

"We don't expect you to go if you don't want," Grace said. "We'd appreciate your carrying us as far as you can, though."

"What if I said this was as far as I was going?" Steve said.

"That would be it then," Grace said.

"You'd walk through this stuff at night?"

"I would," Grace said.

"I'm not crazy about that part," Bob said. "I might even be talked out of it. I might even ride back with you the other way."

"You?" Steve asked me.

"All that matters right now," I said, "is are you going to the end or not. If you go back, you know what you've got."

"Sounds like I have a pretty good idea of what I'm gonna get if I go forward too." He looked hard at me. "Tell you what else, I think if I go back and Bob here goes with me, you'll go too. You don't look like any kind of hero to me. The gal here will keep walking, I can tell that. She doesn't think she needs much of anybody."

"That's not true," Grace said. "I can use all the help I can get. But if I don't get it, I'm going on."

"I'm no knight in white armor, lady," Steve said.

"Never crossed my mind you might be."

Steve smiled and put the cigar back in his mouth. He still didn't light it.

"All right, I'll haul you on, but maybe we ought to come up with a game plan. And first thing to start with is getting rid of the old boy in the trunk. He's starting to stink all the way from the back. It bothers my driving. I don't figure we'll have to eat him, with all this fruit and stuff out there, so let's get shed of him."

6

I got Crier's legs and Bob got him by the shoulders and we lifted him out of the Plymouth's trunk. He had swollen up a bit, and he really did stink.

We carried him over to the side of the road and put him down. I said, "I told him I wouldn't do this. I promised I'd get him to the end of the highway."

"Me too," Bob said, "but a person doesn't always get what they want, and you can't always keep your promise. Besides, if he'd known he was gonna stink like this, maybe he wouldn't have asked it of us."

Crier's dick had come out of his pocket and rolled up next to the spare, and since it was past the handling stage, and looked like a big jalapeño going to rot, Steve got a couple of sticks and scissored it out of there and carried it over and dropped it next to Crier.

"We ought to bury him," I said.

"Something will just dig him up," Steve said. "And this ground isn't any kind of ground for digging. But if you want, there's a worn-down spot over there and we can throw him off in that, maybe find something to cover him up, for all that amounts to."

We carried Crier over to the worn-down spot and put

him in it. He was stiff as a tire iron and lay there in the indentation as if he had fallen sideways out of a chair and frozen. Steve kicked the dick on over and into the hole and we got some brush and limbs and the few rocks we could find, and put them on top of him. We got everything covered but the bottom of his shoes. Our hands sure did smell bad.

We got in the car and drove away. Bob said, "I guess we could have at least put his dick in his pocket."

7

All over the place were these TVs and antennas and papers, and the darker it got the more those papers came and swirled and collected in the trees with the film, which was now thicker than the leaves.

Over to the right, just above the trees, you could see what looked like an inverted tornado dipping down, and all of its swirls were filled with posters and bags and stuff. And on the ground were lots of TV sets. It was like we were getting closer to the garbage dump.

It got darker and we kept driving, but now we had all the windows up because the paper storm had really gotten bad, and it somehow seemed safer from the ghosts that way, even if they weren't really dangerous.

All along the highway were people impaled on antennas, and the headlights would wink at the metal between their legs, and sometimes you could see blood and shit on the antennas. But more often you didn't, and as we looked closer, we saw why. There were few real people impaled. Most of what was there were dummies.

A thing I couldn't put a name to began to move in the back of my mind, but whatever was crawling back there went away when I saw what was in the distance.

The Orbit, its tall tin fence sparkling in the lightning flashes like a woman's wedding band catching the fire from a candlelight dinner.

From that distance, it looked like the crumbled remains of an old castle, way the shadows fell over and moved around on it, way the lightning popped and fizzled overhead, way the paper and posters swirled around and into it like ghosts heading home.

We pulled off the road near one of the impaled dummies, turned off the lights, and talked about it.

"Seems to me," Steve said, "driving on in isn't the answer, not if it's like you say it is, Grace."

"That's how he said it was, though he called it a kind of church."

"This is your show," Bob said. "What do you want to do? Tell us, and then I'll tell you if I'll do it."

"Wait until morning. Let me sleep on it. Turn the car around and pull off near the trees on the other side, and take turns at watch. That way nobody comes up on us. In the morning I'll know what to do."

"In other words," Bob said, "you'll be ready to do something even if it's wrong?"

"Pretty much," Grace said. "One of you guys take first watch." She leaned against her side of the car and closed her eyes and went to sleep, or pretended to.

"Yes, Commandant," Bob said.

"Once they got the right to vote, it's been downhill ever since," Steve said.

"I heard that," Grace said.

We guys tried to talk for a while, but we didn't really have anything to talk about. We knew Steve's life story. I took the first watch and we took turns doing that all night, and the last watch was Grace's, I think, because I'd come awake from time to time and see who was on duty. Anyway, next thing I knew it was morning and Grace had the door open and was dumping some fruit in my lap.

It wasn't good fruit. It was kind of sour, but I ate it anyway, and lots of it. I looked at the morning and thought it looked pretty fresh, more real than usual. The papers had stopped swirling and the film lay in the trees and on the ground like burnt bacon.

Grace, Bob and Steve were over by one of the dummies and Steve had a stick and was poking it. I got out of the car and went over there.

Bob said, "Popalong sure works to make things look scary. Speaking of scary, you look like hell."

"Thanks."

"We sort of got us a game plan," Steve said. "Or rather Grace has one."

"All right," I said, "let me hear it."

It wasn't complicated. It went like this. We'd wait until near dark, then start toward the Orbit, going along the edge of the jungle until we got around on the left-hand side of the place and could work around to the back, then climb up on the fence and have a look over. After that, we could play it by ear. Locate Sue Ellen, go in there and nab her and get out of there. As for Popalong, Grace said, "Don't worry about him none. I'll take care of him, come hell or high water."

Thing was, it was going to be night by the time we did what we wanted to do (provided we were able to do it), and coming back to the car was going to be some kind of dreadful, what with that blood-sucking film and those storms out there, not to mention the shadows and the ghosts which, though harmless, didn't do much for the disposition.

Still, it was the only plan we had, simple as it was.

We whiled away the day eating fruit, then when it

started getting windy and the sun started its plunge, we got to walking.

It turned out to be a longer hike than it looked like, and by the time we were at the edge of the Orbit, it was dark and the film was moving.

Steve had the scissors from his shaving kit, and he used that to do some snipping, but we finally had to get away from the jungle, and more out in the clear, so as to stay ahead of the stuff.

There didn't seem to be anyone on sentry duty, and the closer we got the more dummies and real people there were on the antenna poles. The air was full of the odor of rotting bodies and spoiled candy and stale soft drinks.

We went around the edge of the fence and worked our way toward the back, and as we went, we could hear the sounds of television—laugh tracks and voices—and the thought of actually seeing Popalong began to get to me.

Around back, I got Grace up on my shoulders and she looked over the fence, sat there on my shoulders for a while, taking it in.

"Well," Bob said.

"I'll be goddamned," Grace said.

I put her down then and made Bob let me up on his shoulders. I was goddamned too.

What I saw was this vast circle of people gathering around this throne made of television sets, and on the throne was Popalong, the flickerings of some show or another throbbing on his face. And below him and to the left, on another throne of busted sets, was a young girl with her long hair loose. Sue Ellen, I figured.

At the bottom of the double throne were two men. They sat on televisions, well out in front of those behind them. They had ringside seats. I took them for two of the four thugs that had helped Popalong capture Grace and her friends.

But the thing that got to me were the people. You see, from where I was you could get a good view of that part of the lot, and after my eyes had adjusted and I'd taken in the scene, I began to realize that most of the people were pregnant women. There were a few men, but not many. Most of the crowd was not a crowd at all.

Dummies tied to antennas. Lobby cards of actors. Posters with pictures of men and women on them wrapped around stacked television sets. A skeleton here and there with clothes on, or a skull stuck on top of a speaker.

The truth was, Popalong didn't really have many followers. Perhaps he had exaggerated to Grace to sound impressive, or maybe many of them were decorating the poles along the way, or had been eaten.

Didn't his followers demand constant entertainment? What was *Father Knows Best* compared to a public burning? And even if that burning was filmed and shown again and again, could it suffice? New things needed to be filmed and shown so they could be made real. Then fresh realities had to be created. Time after time after time.

Popalong and his followers seemed to be killing themselves out of an audience. The harder Popalong worked for ratings, the fewer people he had to poll.

I got down and Bob and Steve had looks, then we huddled. Grace went over first and I followed. Then Bob. Bob got on my shoulders and gave Steve a hand over.

We began to work our way through the crowd of posters and dummies and skeletons and lobby cards, and sometimes when we came to a real person, they looked at us without curiosity if they looked at us at all; the real stuff was on the TV set.

Grace moved ahead of us, and came out at the front of the crowd and looked up at Popalong.

I saw that Sue Ellen (it had to be her) was dead. Had been for a while. Her face and hands were the color of pee-stained sheets. Her knucklebones punched out of her papery flesh like volcanic eruptions. Her eyes were holes filled with popcorn. One kernel dangled from her left socket like a booger in a nostril.

A tremor went up Grace's back. She yelled at Popalong, "Remember me?"

"It's like a movie," Popalong said. "You coming into my lair."

There was a surge of wind and a mass of paper and popcorn and soft drink slush blew through the drive-in and passed on.

When the wind was gone and the paper had quit rustling, Grace said, "You and this place look all worn out. Your church is light in the pews. I think you're nothing more than a walking TV set with a line of shit."

"It's good of you to come," Popalong said. "Of course, you know what comes next."

The two toughs got up and turned toward Grace. They didn't look as weak as the others. Better diet. More human flesh maybe.

"Good to see you boys," Grace said. "I think about you lots."

The one on Grace's left got to her first. He had a piece of glass wedged into a short stick and he tried to stab her in the stomach.

Before we could make any kind of move to help her, Grace sidestepped the glass, slapped the thug's hand down and kicked him between the eyes so hard his head went back more than his neck allowed. He folded up like an accordion at her feet.

The other tough bolted.

He was a good runner. We didn't chase him. He headed for the exit. He wouldn't last long out there. Not at night, not with the film crawling.

Popalong's followers seemed uncertain. This was the sort of thing they saw a lot of, but in this case it was short and sweet and not nearly melodramatic enough. They shuffled their feet. Maybe they wanted to see it on film.

If any of them had it in their heads to go for Grace, it was an idea that went away when she turned and glared at them.

Popalong's followers were now no more than a pack of pregnant women and skinny men, their brains no better than straw. They might as well have been the dummies that the sky kept raining.

We pushed to the front. I looked up at Popalong. A Western was playing on his face. Just as a Hollywood Indian took a bullet and fell off his horse, Popalong made the tube go black. "You're just a television set," I said. "We can turn you off anytime we want."

Grace grabbed one of the dummies and pulled at it. It came loose of the antenna that held it. She grabbed the antenna and pulled it out of the asphalt and stepped up on the base of the television throne and poked at Popalong with it.

"Come down so I can change your channels," she said. "Come down so I won't have to bring you down. I want to see you come down, King Popalong. Come on down where you belong."

"Stop it," Popalong said. "You fools are ruining things. I've got anything you want to see. There's not a show so exotic that I don't have it. Anything happens to me and you'll be back in darkness. You'll have to talk to entertain yourselves."

Grace poked him again. He stood up. She poked his knee and his knee buckled and he went down and tried to get up again, but the knee twisted under him and he came tumbling down the sets. As he went, he grabbed out and got hold of Sue Ellen's hand. She came off her throne and tumbled after him.

Popalong hit with a crunch and a smash of glass. Sue Ellen lay on top of him.

Popalong tried to get his hands underneath him. Steve went over and straddled him and pulled Sue Ellen off, then took the guns out of Popalong's holster and stepped back.

Popalong folded his knees under him and lifted his body upright. A chunk of glass fell out of his face. There was a gap dead center of the set and dozens of hairline fractures went out from it. The entire thing pulsed like an asshole straining to shit. Something sparked in the ruined depths, and the sparks jumped about like little red rats trying to abandon ship.

He tried to get up again, but his legs weren't having it. A rope of smoke twisted out of the hole in his face and rose up. The rabbit ears under his hat pushed it back and felt the air, as if searching for signals. But nothing was on that face but wreckage.

The rabbit ears went away and the hat fell back into place.

"It's all over now," Grace said, and started forward.

I grabbed her elbow. "That's enough."

"Not hardly," she said.

"Don't be his high priestess," I said. "You're giving him a TV or movie ending. Kind where the wronged person deals out revenge on the bad guy. He's too messed up to be a bad guy. He's pathetic. He's out of it, through. Don't martyr him for yourself and these people. It won't do a thing for Timothy or Sue Ellen."

"It's not like he's got anything left to hurt anyone with," Bob said.

"Guess you got two cents to put in on this, Steve," Grace said.

"It was me, I'd take him out. Hell, I'll shoot him for you if you like. It won't bother me none. But this is your show. You name the channel."

Grace looked at Popalong's ruptured face, at the scrawny body that held up the massive head, the black cowboy suit that hung off of him like a kid wearing daddy's clothes.

She went over and picked up Sue Ellen and walked away. Popcorn dribbled out of Sue Ellen's eye sockets, sprinkled the ground like snow.

Steve sighed. "This is kind of disappointing. Kind of like a cowboy movie without a final showdown, ain't it?"

"It's exactly like that," I said.

DISSOLVE TO:

Epilogue

We used some of the drier pieces of cardboard and paper we could find and built a mound and put Sue Ellen on it and covered her with some more pieces. Then Steve lit it with a match he'd found in one of the derelict cars, and after a while, most of Sue Ellen was cremated. What was left over we scooped up in Coke cups and took it off in the woods and tossed it around.

Popalong's dead bodyguard was hauled off during all the commotion by one of the drive-in people, and I guess he got eaten.

Next morning, we went to look for Crier's body. It was gone. Something had dug him out. Whatever it was got his dick too.

As for Popalong, in time he crawled back up that stack of TVs and found his place on the throne. He sat there with his tongue of blue and red wires hanging out and the inside of his face popping sparks and fizzling from time to time. But finally that quit.

He grew thin inside that cowboy suit, and when the flesh went away, there were no bones in him, just cable wires and rods of antenna held together with tightly wrapped film.

Steve brought his car into the drive-in, and he and Grace took up together and went to living out of it. I tell you, I never expected that to happen. Maybe all those bangs Grace got on the head had clouded her sense of judgment.

Bob and I built our place out of TV sets. Walls and ceiling. We used antenna pieces and part of an old car to make it work. In the mornings we wake up and watch Grace come out of the Plymouth and do her martial arts exercises. In the nude.

The bending over stuff is dynamite.

She's got a big round tummy now. She says I didn't pull out fast enough and the baby's mine. She says it's pretty far along, but isn't showing much because she's tall. Since I didn't eat the King's popcorn and neither did she, she thinks the baby has a good chance to be healthy. I don't know how I feel about that.

The other women have had their babies and—

Yes, I'm talking about you guys. But hold up, I'm almost through here. Just be polite and let me get through this.

—they look like the Popcorn King. Two bodies welded together, one on the other's shoulders, to make a single unit. Unlike the King, they are covered in eyes. The eyes look like the eyes that were on the corn the King puked up. Each eye blinks at a different time. I feel like I'm constantly receiving Morse code.

They're all sexless. I mean there's no equipment that I can see. Keeps from having to wipe a lot of asses. They came out of the cannon practically walking. They can put simple sentences together already. They're almost as tall as me. They like to listen to me read, and though they under-

stand a lot of the words, a lot of sentences, I don't think
they get the gist of it all—

*Okay, Leroy. I take it back. You do understand. That's
all for today, guys, girls, whatever. Go find a car to tear
up. I was kidding about there being a test at the end of
this. . . .*

What test?

Forget it, Leroy. Bye now.

That was about all I had written. I'm back inside the
hut now and I'm sitting here finishing this out as best I can,
which is just as well. I'm running out of things to write
with. I've looked everywhere, glove boxes, the concession
stand over in B lot, you name it. I've written this in pen and
pencil, crayon and eyeliner.

But it doesn't matter, I'm also running out of things to
say. I guess I can mention that the mothers of those kids, or
whatever they are, don't love them. But I'm not sure that's
all their fault. How can they be mothers after all they've
seen and done?

I see some of the drive-in people looking up at the
corpse of Popalong, almost wistfully, I think. At night they
wander about in the storms, nothing to do. They've forgotten how to talk to one another. It's a good thing those weird
kids were born practically grown.

Sometimes I take the kids hunting with me. They
chase down the game on foot. Bob says he thinks he saw
one throw a stick without touching it the other day. Kid just
willed it up and there it went, hit a rabbit in the back of the
head and killed it.

Bob admits he saw this out of the corner of his eye, and
it may not be like that, but I wouldn't be surprised.

Well, like I said we hunt a lot. Thought a better diet

might help the people here, help them get a better frame of mind. But all it does is help them get around faster.

Sometimes I think I'll start back down the highway, but I'd have to go on foot and I don't like the idea of those storms or that film out there at night. Still, I think about it. Shit Town might be a better life than this. Hell, getting back to Jungle Home wouldn't be too bad.

Let's see . . . Oh yeah, Grace has a shadow now, and Steve is starting to have one. Bob and I still don't. I'm not sure what this means, but it worries me a little, especially when I see Grace working out and popping the air with her punches, and right behind her, capering like a chimp, making fun of her moves, is her shadow. Maybe I'll stop getting up in the morning to watch her. That shadow takes the joy out of it.

Bob and I have talked about having the kids get some TV sets and start them stacking them, help us rebuild one of those pyramids Popalong had his followers burn down. If what Popalong says is true, we could go up there and have a look around.

But maybe that's not such a good idea. It's only in Hollywood movies that the afflicted are always able to get the nasty aliens and twist their tentacles behind their backs and make them return things to normal.

I figure if we go up there nothing will work out the way we want. We could get done to us what was done to Popalong, or worse. And unlike Popalong, it isn't something we'd like to happen.

It's hard to know what to do next. Life is like that Max Brand book the guy in Shit Town was talking about. There's always a couple of pages torn out, so you don't know how it's going to end.

Still, I'm a sucker for a happy ending. Hell, I used to believe in God and astrology. So I'm going to give myself a happy ending even if I don't get one in real life. The best ending that comes to mind is what that person wrote on the inside back cover of that book. It may not be the truth for any of us, but like the fella said, you can't really think of anything better than that.

So lie or not, here goes:

He rode off into the West and everything was okay.

ABOUT THE AUTHOR

JOE R. LANSDALE is a full-time writer and a lifelong resident of East Texas. He is the author of two novels and more short stories than anyone wants to count. He generally writes Western, Science Fiction, Mysteries, Horror and Fantasy and has appeared in most of the genre magazines. His most recent Doubleday books are an award-winning anthology *Best of the West* and a Double D Western novel, *The Magic Wagon*. He has published *The Drive-In* with Bantam Spectra. Mr. Lansdale lives in East Texas with his wife and son.